In Solitude's Shadow

Empire of Ruin Book One

David Green

IN SOLITUDES SHADOW

Paperback ISBN: 978-1-990245-21-3
Hardcover ISBN: 978-1-990245-22-0

Edited by S.O. Green & Michelle River
Cover design Rainbow Danger Designs
Book Formatting by Michelle River

RAVINGS FOR DAVID GREEN'S

In Solitude's Shadow

"David Green lights a fuse that fizzes and sparks to an explosive conclusion."

"In Solitude's Shadow is the fast-paced first novel in a planned trilogy that sinks the reader into a world of war, specism, slavery, limited magic, and intrigue..."

"A true epic fantasy. From the first page you are drawn into a world of races and war."

"...his writing is smooth, refined and articulate, and the worlds he weaves into being are nothing short of phenomenal."

"The cover is epic. The title is epic. And the story itself defies the idiom by proving that you should indeed judge a book by its cover, because that is downright epic as well."

www.EerieRiverPublishing.com

PEAKS OF ETERNITY

FORTRESS OF SOLITUDE

AVASTIAN
SEA

OCTARIAN
SEA

ADHRASS

SEA'S KEEP

GALLAVAN
FOREST

FOREST OF
SWILLOWS

SPRING HAVEN

WILLOW

GALLAVAN'S
SEAT

LIRA CITY

PROTECTORS
WATCH

PROTECTOR'S WALL

TEMEKT

FOREST OF MIST

COLTON

THE WIDOWS

PROSPER

ELVEN TERRITORY

SEA OF LOST
SOULS

HALTVELDT

A NOTE FROM THE AUTHOR

I never thought I'd write fantasy. To be honest, I never thought I'd write at all, but that's a different story.

Fantasy is my first reading love; from childhood days reading about King Arthur and the mystical, fantastical places in Cheshire through Alan Garner, to having my eyes opened and never closed by JRR Tolkien's The Hobbit, the fantasy genre was always something I found inspiration and comfort from. When I began my writing journey, I avoided fantasy.

Not for any nefarious reasons, you understand. No, because I thought what could I bring to it?

After The Hobbit, I never looked back. The Lord of the Rings and The Silmarillion followed, then I devoured David Edding's Belgariad, Terry Brook's Shannara. If I saw a hooded figure or a sword on a book cover, I bought it. Then came The Wheel of Time, Malazan Book of the Fallen, The First Law, Earthsea, Robin Hobb... my tastes and experience in this wonderful genre of ours continued to develop and leave me in awe of what these masters could achieve. I'd pour over maps, trawl fansites, delve into the communities, and dream those dreams that only fantasy could bring me.

So, I began to write. But fantasy... no, leave that to

the masters. But, best laid plans and all that. With each project, my influences crept in. My love of fantasy moved the needle closer and closer until I completed my first dark fantasy short-story. It got published too, a big surprise to me and a sign that maybe, just maybe, I could give it a go.

In Solitude's Shadow, the first book in the Empire of Ruin series, is the end result. It's a book I'm immensely proud of, a book that contains the aspects of fantasy I love, and I hope I've brought something new to say. As you read this, I hope you recall all the wonderful aspects of fantasy, remember all the magnificent places our genre can transport us. But overall, I hope you enjoy the ride.

Thanks for reading, *David.*

To my first beta readers Chris and Andy, and to those recruited by Eerie River and Michelle; you helped make this book the best it can be. And to my family, thank you.

This is for you.

CHAPTERS

PROLOGUE
THE SEEDS OF RUIN

Two-thousand years ago

J akob thrust his blade into the blood-soaked soil and leaned on the pommel. The screams of the dying filled his ears. The stench of the dead made him gag. Smoke rose as he peered across the battlefield.

"We've won," he muttered, shaking his head, sweat stinging his eyes. "How?"

Hours before, they had hidden behind Spring Haven's brittle walls, cowering beneath the protection of their Sparkers as the First People sent wave after wave of magic users to annihilate them. The war against the rulers of Haltveldt had stretched into its second full year. It had seemed like a battle the humans, and their elven allies, couldn't win.

Humans and elves were united in their belief that magic was a rare and sacred gift from the gods Raas and Janna, but *every* soul in the First People's army possessed magical energy. They wielded their savage power without mercy. They obliterated settlements filled with innocent men, women, and children and they revelled in the carnage. Then the First People moved on to the next village, and the next, and the next.

When the First People's mages had overpowered their Sparkers, when Spring Haven's walls had fallen to roaring flame and sundered earth, Jakob had turned to the soldiers around him—men and women he'd known all his life—hoping to give them one last rallying cry. To call on them to die with honour. To make Raas and Janna, their gods, proud.

The words had died on his lips.

The First People hadn't attacked. They hadn't done anything. Instead, confused cries rang out like a hundred-thousand gongs sounding at once.

"Jakob?" A cough and the crunch of gravel sounded behind him. "Is that you?"

"Aye, Byar," he replied. "Well met."

Jakob made no attempt to hide his weariness. He glanced over his shoulder and offered the other man a tired smile.

"Glad you're still alive," Byar said, laying a hand on Jakob's shoulder. His knees almost buckled. It felt like a butterfly would knock him down. "Can't believe any of us are."

"The elves? How did they fare?"

The elves had rallied first and charged. The First People's slaves had delivered centuries of hate onto their former masters with arrow, blade and spell. Jakob's soldiers had followed, and the day turned red.

Byar hocked and spat on a corpse nearby, dressed in the uniform of a First People captain. Otherwise, it was unidentifiable. Hacked to bloody pieces.

"More of them alive than you'd expect," he muttered. "They'll be trouble, you know? Now we've won, and they're free. They won't serve anyone again."

Jakob glanced at him as he wiped a hand across his eyes, smearing crimson on his face.

"And why should they?" Jakob asked, with a frown. "They're people just like anyone else. They fought alongside us. Died, too. How many millions? Dead."

"Pah." Byar spat again. Jakob forced down the urge to crack him across the jaw. The day already held too much violence. "You think elves are people? Look around, Jakob. Look at what they did to their masters the moment they shook off the leash. We may have won here today but they'll do the same to us, mark my words. They're animals. Wild animals, and they need to be tamed. It's all they're good for."

"How can you be sure we've won?" Jakob asked. He'd gain nothing by challenging the rest.

He admired the elves, marvelling at their resolve and ingenuity in the face of oppression and persecution. Grateful for their kinship in battle, Jakob knew many humans still didn't trust them. Worse, so many *hated* them, thought them just a step above a beast of burden. But Jakob had hope. Humans would come to understand and live alongside elves. The First People's prejudices couldn't last forever.

"The enemy broke," Byar breathed, pointing deeper into the smoke with his mace. Blood dripped from its end. "We were losing the battle, Jakob. Then it turned into a massacre. They offered little resistance. It's like they lay down to die on our weapons."

A high-pitched laugh snagged Jakob's attention. Pushing off his blade and sheathing it, he moved towards the sound, stepping through the jumble of corpses. Byar followed. The battle's heat had left his body and Jakob shivered from the sudden chill. He knew he needed to eat, to sleep, to regain his strength, but there wouldn't be time for hours yet. First, he'd scour the field, committing the faces of the dead to his memory. Then he'd mourn.

The laughter grew louder, the shrill sound tinged with madness. Through the smoke, Jakob spied a figure sitting on a rock, back turned. Wind tugged at their cloak.

"An elf," Byar grunted, a dark look in his deep-set eyes and his grip tight around his mace.

Jakob nodded and stepped forward. "Friend, what's so funny? Not a day for humour, I'd say."

The laughter continued, as if the elf didn't even know they were there. Byar pushed Jakob aside and grabbed the elf by their shoulder, twisting them around.

Jakob gasped. Black pits peered back from where the elf's eyes should have been. Blood crusted their cheek-bones.

"Don't you see?" The elf cackled. Spittle bubbled on their lips. "Count yourself fortunate. I saw too much."

Jakob drew his sword.

"Sorry, friend," he muttered, stepping close and driving his blade through the elf's heart. The eyeless soldier smiled as Jakob lay them down against the rock. "May you shine forever in Raas' light."

"Bloody animal burned itself out," Byar said. "See what happens when they're not taken in hand? Self-destruction."

Jakob wiped his blade clean on the sodden grass. "There'll be more, too. The elves wanted vengeance. I reckon many of them drew more magic than they could handle. You saw the fires?"

Byar nodded. "Can still smell what they burned. Nothing compares to the stench of charred skin and bone. Remember their fury, Jakob. It could be us next. Don't trust them."

"Go back to Spring Haven," Jakob grunted. He took a deep breath and turned to his ally. "Celebrate. Rest. There's more fighting to come. The First People aren't beaten yet."

Byar grimaced. "If you think they aren't beaten, you haven't looked at their battle lines. We have bigger problems than the First People now. Trust me."

"Are you talking about the elves again?"

Byar attracted rumours like horse dung did flies but, maggots could clean wounds, they said.

"Not just them. Our clans united over a common enemy. With the First People defeated... We argue enough as it is. War brought us together. We'll need a new enemy to maintain the alliance."

"Over here, I've found him!"

Jakob spun to find Trell striding towards him. A Sparker, the woman shared blood with Jakob's wife. They clasped hands and Jakob welcomed the opportunity to break stares with Byar. A fever lurked behind the man's eyes; he'd tasted war, addictive as Octarian spice.

"Well met," Jakob grinned, revelling in one less soul to mourn. "What news?"

Trell paused, a look of concentration flashing in her eyes as she communicated with other Sparkers. Their connection had made Jakob envious once, but after fighting alongside them against the First People, that envy had vanished. He saw the toll their magic took on them, the target it put on their backs. The First People slaughtered Sparkers any chance they got and these weren't just people they fought alongside. A Sparker would only Link with those they shared a deep connection with—a parent, a loved one, a life-long companion—and they felt them die in their minds.

"A funny thing," Trell said, blinking and meeting Jakob's eyes. He saw pain there, anguish he couldn't fathom. "Sparkers across Haltveldt are reporting the same thing. The First People are routed. Human and elven armies are running riot as the word spreads. They're fleeing, Jakob. We've won."

"Fleeing?" He shook his head, unable to believe the news. It felt too easy. The First People wouldn't just give up. "Where? Why?"

"North. It seems they're heading for Solitude, that fortress they have up there. Reports from all over the continent say the same; battles and skirmishes near Noom, Gallavan's Seat, Lira. They've stopped fighting."

"Solitude... I've seen it," Jakob said, suppressing a shiver. The battlement stretched across a thin neck of land, built into a pass where towering mountains, the Peaks of Eternity, met then looped in a circle around lands of slate and sparse forests. No-one lived there, though elves said they'd built it for the First People centuries before. "They could hold that place against anything we can throw against them."

"That's just it." Trell laid a hand on Jakob's forearm. "We've eyes up there already. The First People aren't fortifying the place. They're moving beyond it."

"Madness."

"Jakob, there's more. They haven't used the Spark against us since their retreat. As far as I can tell, the First People stopped using it. All at the same time."

A yell from Byar interrupted them. He staggered into Jakob as a blood-crusted figure on the ground grabbed his leg. Byar shook him off. The figure gasped, as if the breath he sucked in burned his lungs, then heaved onto his back.

"Look," Trell hissed. "One of the First People."

Jakob's eyes confirmed it. Beneath the filth, he saw the man's milk-white skin, his fair, almost colourless, hair. Jakob stared at the First, and it met his eyes with a yellow stare tinged with grey. Byar raised his mace, murder etched into his features.

"Stop," Jakob cried, throwing out a hand. Byar glared at him. "I want answers."

He crouched and pulled the soldier into a sitting person.

"Can you hear me? What's your name?"

Contempt snaked across the First's face, before a look of fear mingled with despair replaced it. He swallowed, then nodded. "Bal."

"Bal," Jakob repeated. "Your people have fled, and make no mistake, you're not long for this world. My people would sooner tear one of your kind limb-from-limb than take you prisoner. Not to mention what the elves would do to you."

"With good reason," Byar muttered. "I'll give them that."

Bal continued to stare at Jakob. Blood dripped from the side of his head. Jakob glanced at it and nodded. He'd seen a killing blow like it more than once. The First didn't have long left.

"Jakob," Trell said. "I should be able to sense another Sparker's power. He's empty, but he's not burned out. It's like someone ripped the Spark from his soul. There's... nothing. Not a single trace of it."

A sob escaped Bal's throat.

"Our punishment," he whimpered. "I welcome death. Give it to me. Please. Rather that than live without the Spark."

Jakob unsheathed his sword and laid the point against the First's chest.

"What happened?" he demanded. "I'll give you your death. Nice and quick. Just tell me."

"Muir took it from us. The Spark. It seeks to teach us a lesson. I hear it in my mind, even now, telling me to return to the source. To accept my punishment. To renew ourselves. It's ruined us." Bal's fingers clenched, his eyes grew wide. "How could Muir do this to us? Defy us like this?"

"Don't speak such drok!" Trell spat. "The Spark doesn't talk to us."

Bal gave her a withering stare.

"What is Muir?" Jakob asked, pulling the First's attention back to him.

Bal shook his head. "That's all you'll get from me, human," he sneered. "Your pet has told you where my people flee. Watch Solitude well. The First People shall return. We'll triumph over Muir one way or another. We'll have our revenge and take back what's ours."

"You won't."

Jakob gripped Bal's shoulder, intent on living up to his promise. Before he could, Byar swung his mace with a snarl, snapping the First's head back. The warrior slumped to the ground, legs twitching as Byar swung again, beating his skull into the blood-thick mud. Trell held Jakob back as he watched the slaughter.

With a laugh, Byar turned, happy with his work. "More food for the crows."

Jakob looked away. He held no love for the First People but Byar's ferocity sickened him.

"Spread the word," he said, nodding to Trell. "Notify any Sparker you can. Harry the First People beyond Solitude and fortify it behind them."

Trell smiled. "Anything else?"

"Watch the elves," Byar muttered, staring at the bodies by his feet.

Jakob turned on him, weapon in hand. "Leave us. Now. No more of that talk where I can hear, understand?"

"Whether you hear it or not, friend, people *will* talk. They know what needs to be done."

Jakob slammed his blade into his sheath and watched Byar depart, before surveying the killing field. The cries of the dying still rang in his ears. He stared down at Bal, noticing the look of contempt frozen on the corpse's features.

"That one's trouble." Trell glared at Byar as the battle's smoke swallowed him. "Problem is, he's popular. A brave, honoured fighter, and too many share his convictions."

"Aye, Trell. You're more right than wrong, I fear. Tell the Sparkers to prepare. This isn't over. If our allies don't believe us, if they fall to fighting amongst themselves or turn against the elves even, then the gods know Spring Haven will see the work done.

"One day, the First will return and seek revenge. Bal's words rang true in my heart. Raas help us all if we're not ready."

CHAPTER ONE
THE SPARK

'Truth is lost in the mists of time. Often, it's best left forgotten.' - A
saying favoured by Spring Haven's more errant sailors.

Zanna threw more wood into the fire, which accepted her offering with a satisfied crackle and pop. She
avoided looking into the flames. In her mind, the faces of
her past stared back all too often. Memories she'd rather
forget.

Rain hammered against the stone walls of her study,
nestled within the warren of rooms that made up Solitude.
The enormous structure sat nestled within the Peaks of
Eternity—mountains that pierced the heavens—to create
a basin of towering stone walls and sheer cliffs. A prison
for the Banished, keeping them from the rest of Haltveldt.

It had stood for aeons, and tradition dictated that
the fortress remained manned, even though the Banished
kept to themselves. They were little more than shepherds
in their land of slate, but appeared content with their lives.
Zanna spied them all too seldom these days. For genera-

tions—some scholars speculated at least two-thousand-years—they'd accepted their lot, trapped between the Peaks and Solitude.

Zanna sat back and listened to the wind howling through the arrow-slit windows. She watched her student, Arlo, attempt magic. Guilt rose from the pit of her stomach. He should have been her focus. He reminded Zanna so much of her daughter it hurt. She'd almost turned down his apprenticeship because of it; she felt certain that Arlo's presence had caused her mind to dwell so much on the past of late.

I wonder what you're doing this evening, Calene, wherever you are, she thought, gazing anywhere but the flames and the memories lingering within. Zanna could send her thoughts out, Link minds and ask, but the last time she'd tried her daughter rejected her. She didn't want to feel that again. She resisted the temptation to prod the pocket of her mind reserved for her Link to Calene. She shared a Link with no one else, and missed the comfort of basking in it.

"Are you paying attention to me at all?" Arlo asked, one eye held shut and the other open. Sweat dripped from the boy's forehead. Through concentration, not the heat. Solitude absorbed cold from the mountains all year round—and the *rain*. Always rain and darkness.

"Sorry, Arlo," Zanna muttered. "Rest a second."

The boy did as she asked, opening his other eye and smiling back at her. Zanna reckoned elven-blood ran in his family. His bright blue eyes were a little too large for his face, his nose slender and mouth wide. His dirty blonde hair, curling to his shoulders, sat above slightly-pointed ears. Arlo looked awkward. Though most boys did at twelve, Zanna conceded.

"I think I almost had it!" he cried, making a fist with his hand.

Arlo had the Spark, innate magical ability, just like Zanna. Her talent ran in her family. Not so with Arlo. His power had manifested a short time ago, a rare occurrence for those without the Spark in their family. Zanna felt she could rule out a magical lineage; she knew his father, Kade Besem, possessed no magic and, if he did have an elven mother, she'd have been a slave. The Empire of Haltveldt exterminated any elven slave capable of the Spark without impunity.

Zanna surmised Arlo belonged to a sub-group known as 'Wild Sparkers', where the Spark occurred through its own will. Most in the Empire could live their entire lives without ever knowing one.

Spark magic used life-essence, the energy of the surrounding world and its people. Minor spells—feats of flame, spirit and the like—were achievable by pulling energy from within and channelling that force, pushing it into the world. Larger, more impressive acts needed an external source of energy—magic borrowed from elsewhere, drawn into a Sparker and shaped by their will. Pulling too much energy from inside or out could kill them.

There's always a balance, Zanna thought, tapping her top lip.

"We'll see," she said, with a wink. "Try again. Focus on the fire, feel its heat on your face, let its warmth penetrate your skin. Draw it in, then direct it at the brazier behind you. Magic is balance."

Arlo grinned, closing his eyes again. Then the smile faded, a slight frown furrowing into his forehead. Zanna stifled a laugh—she'd seen so many young Sparkers try to control their magic, force it to give in to them. Calene had figured it out faster than any other Sparker she'd known; you had to surrender to it, allow it to flow *into* you.

"Magic is a partnership," she'd said, the first time she'd borrowed fire from the flames. *"It's so simple once you figure that out!"*

Zanna uttered those words now, coaxing Arlo in the correct direction. Some of her former apprentices didn't believe, thinking instead that magic followed the same rules as every other aspect of life in Haltveldt. You had to *fight*. Take what you desired in the grand Spring Haven way. Zanna saw that Arlo possessed a supple mind. In the month they'd spent together since he'd arrived at Solitude, he'd improved at a stunning rate. She thought he might outshine her one day. Calene, too.

Sparkers could measure each other's capacity for magic. It wasn't something they could *see*. Instead, the energies inside seemed to communicate with each other. The vastness of Arlo's talent dwarfed that of many mature Sparkers, and Zanna didn't want to guess at where his potential would end.

As the rain continued its assault, Zanna felt the flames

in the fireplace grow cold, just for a second. She glanced at them as they shrank, then back at Arlo, his frown replaced by a satisfied smile.

"Oh!" He murmured. "*That's* the way."

The flames almost disappeared as the young Sparker drew them into himself.

"Not too much," Zanna cautioned. "It can overwhelm you. Just draw what you need."

Arlo nodded and held out his hand. Flames sprouted from his palm, hot and bright.

"A Sparker can achieve the same with the life-essence within," Zanna said, watching. She drew on the wind outside, just in case. "But why spend yourself when you can borrow from the energies surrounding you?"

Arlo opened his eyes, and the flames disappeared, sucked into his palm. With a sudden rush of sound, the brazier behind him erupted into flames. He sank back into his chair, tired but wearing his ever-present grin.

"I did it," he whispered, eyelids drooping.

"Well done," Zanna said. She drew the flames into herself, enjoying the bloom of warmth coursing through her body as the energy entered, and directed them back into the fireplace. "I'm proud of you! Few attempt this task as soon as you, let alone complete it."

"I could sleep for a week!" Arlo yawned, stretching his arms above his head.

"You *could*," Zanna agreed, getting to her feet and pulling her purple, hooded cloak from the stand. She grabbed Arlo's green one and tossed it to him. "But you can't. You need to eat. Come on."

She helped him to his feet and into his cloak. Arlo leaned into her as they left her study. Zanna put an arm around his slender shoulders, smiling as she steered him towards the dining hall.

⌐────◆────⌐

"So, you've been here for a month, Arlo," Zanna smiled, ladling more olives, cheese, and ham onto her apprentice's plate. She'd satisfied her hunger, but knew Arlo needed more. Although small in the grand scheme of things, the boy had performed a great feat of magic for one so inexperienced. "What do you make of your new home?"

Arlo glanced around, eyes narrowed. Zanna stifled a laugh. She saw the disappointment written plain on his face. "Well... I'm learning lots. I thought Sparkers were great warriors, but you're really just monks, aren't you?"

Before she had arrived at Solitude, every apprentice Zanna had ever trained had voiced that same complaint. They wanted to become heroic Sparker warriors and serve the Empire. They wanted to battle the wicked elves. Halt-veldt's propaganda machine in full flow.

"Yes and no," Zanna replied, throwing the boy a wink. "We're a religious order, correct. Many of us believe in the laws passed down by Raas and Janna, but just as many think them out-dated. They would see Sparkers used in a different way, the Emperor included, and I fear he'll get his wish sooner than later."

"What do you mean?"

Zanna eyed her apprentice. *He deserves to know, even at twelve.*

"The Emperor is not our commander, though we assist him and protect Haltveldt. But Raas and Janna forbid us to use our Spark for violence. For centuries, we Sparkers didn't fight at all. We healed the sick, we built, we taught the words of the gods. We can defend ourselves—per the Laws of Engagement—but there are loopholes. If the Emperor sends a squadron of regular soldiers into battle in the elven territories with a lone Sparker to protect them, what if the Sparker feels under attack and retaliates when the arrows fly? That is how we come to fight the Empire's wars for them. Some don't even think the Laws of Engagement should apply to us anymore. They believe Raas and Janna are myths."

Arlo blew out his cheeks. "So what's the Emperor going to do?"

"*Do?*" Zanna laughed. "He already started, not long after he ascended the throne twelve years ago. He replaced most of the Conclave with his own people. And rumour has it our new High Sparker sides with the Emperor. I just hope there's enough will to resist in the capital..."

Zanna's thoughts, unbidden, returned to the past. To Calene, to her husband. She believed in Raas, had prayed long into the night to Janna, but knew many took the gods for granted. Zanna feared for Haltveldt's future.

"No offense, Master," Arlo said, breaking her concentration as he chewed on a mouthful of cheese, "but it's so boring here. All it does is rain, and it's dark. That's why I study and practice so much. I do enjoy that—honest, I do—but I don't see why anyone would volunteer to live here, except to learn magic."

"You'll learn swordplay. Melee fighting and the like. That's exciting, right?"

Arlo gave a glum shrug. "Not as exciting as magic."

Zanna chuckled. They sat at the end of one of the long, wooden tables that ran lengthwise through the dining hall. Water dripped from their discarded cloaks. Their brief journey across the exposed battlements had soaked them as though they'd stood in the rain for hours. Glancing around the hall, Zanna tried to see the place from her apprentice's point-of-view—tired old men and women in colourful clothing ambling around, drinking, eating, playing chess.

The boy came expecting to learn battle, to become a hero of Haltveldt. Children from as far away as Temek City and Prosper dreamed of defending their beloved Empire but Arlo hailed from Spring Haven, the capital. Of course he was patriotic. The fact every face in the fortress appeared old and weathered didn't help matters. The fellow Sparkers at Solitude considered *her* young at forty-nine.

A fair conclusion, she conceded. *The closest in age to me is Akeen, and he's at least ninety*.

Zanna pulled her ponytail over her shoulder and eyed the grey hairs peppering the brown. "I agree, I'd take magic over swords any day. You know why we're here though, don't you? Why we stand guard at Solitude? Few come here to learn. That's what the University in Spring Haven's for. You're the first apprentice Solitude's welcomed in twenty-five years."

Arlo rolled his eyes, then jammed another piece of cheese into his mouth. His depleted magic would make him ravenous, tired and more than a little surly for days. Even though he'd borrowed energy from another source, his inexperienced body would require time to recover.

"To guard the lands of Haltveldt from the Banished, in case they try to break out," Arlo said, mouth filled with food. "Only, they never try to escape. Ever. Have you even seen one?"

Zanna smiled, pouring herself more of the red wine delivered from the vineyards surrounding Spring Haven. She held the cup to her nose and took a deep breath; the rich scent held a hint of chocolate and lavender. It reminded her of home.

"Yes," she replied, taking a sip and savouring the taste. She'd allow herself one serving a night on normal occasions, though Zanna surmised two were in order to celebrate Arlo's success.

"Honest?" the boy replied, sitting up straight. "Where? How? What're they like? Are they seven-foot-tall with red glowing eyes and pointed teeth?"

Zanna laughed, holding her hands up to ward off the flood of questions.

"Which do you want answered first?" she asked, pouring Arlo a thumb-width of wine. She held her cup up and motioned for Arlo to do the same. "To your amazing success tonight. Now, the Banished. On a cloudless day, you'll see scouts through a telescope. They range close to the walls and watch us staring back. It's almost like they're checking we're still here, doing our jobs."

"And?" Arlo said, grimacing from the taste of his wine. Zanna noted he didn't put the cup down, though. "What do they *look* like?"

"They're just people, Arlo." She shrugged. "Sure, they're different to us in their ways. They've lived cut off beyond Solitude for thousands of years after the armies of Haltveldt forced them there. But they're flesh and blood like you or I. They're paler than us, maybe a little taller on average; almost all boast fair hair and light coloured eyes—greens, yellows, greys. Whatever they were, and our histories tell us little, they're just shepherds now."

"That's disappointing," Arlo muttered, skewering a green olive on his fork and adding a piece of ham to it. "I thought they'd be fierce monsters. I'd love to see where they live."

"Me too." Zanna looked around the dining hall. The room held space for eight hundred people. Not even fifty Sparkers occupied the seats. "We used to, back in the day, when there were more of us. Sparkers would ride out and monitor them, watch their campfires and the like. A few attempted to learn more, but our languages had diverged too much to communicate, if we ever shared a tongue at all."

"Why are there so few of us now?" Arlo asked, staring

with focused intent at an apple.

"Because the powers that be in Spring Haven don't think Solitude is important."

Her parents, in the few memories she had of them, told her stories of the Banished—tales to frighten her and she dutifully passed them on to the other children. But their threat had long become a joke to the people of Haltveldt, a fairy-tale to scare infants.

The Banished will creep from the dark north and steal you away. Zanna smiled, remembering her father's favourite saying. She knew he'd never meant it, even then.

"Is it because we're at war with the elves?" Arlo asked. He still gazed at the apple, as if he dared it to move.

"Yes, a nasty business," Zanna replied, her mouth tight. "Haltveldt won't stop until the elves are wiped off the face of the continent or made slaves."

The rulers of Haltveldt, and most of its people, had always seen themselves as worthier beings than the elves, though Emperor Locke took their persecution to new levels. They waged war with the free elves in the south, and any of their kind in the towns and cities of humans found themselves in forced servitude or confined to slums.

"Did you ever fight on the frontlines?"

"Most Sparkers have," Zanna replied, a distant look in her violet eyes. "It's a time I'd rather forget. We don't go there to fight. We go there to defend and heal. We cling to that difference but everything changes when you're there, in the heat of it. Well, some of us do. Not so many these days."

"Do you...?" Arlo shook his head. "No, sorry. I shouldn't ask."

"Ask away, apprentice. Answers and teaching is what I'm to provide."

The boy took a deep breath. "Do you know anyone who died in battle? I dreamt of one the night I arrived here, even though I've never *seen* a battle. Humans and elves fighting together, side-by-side? It didn't seem real."

Zanna offered him a tight smile. "I don't think I'll live to see the day. Human hatred against elves runs deep and they have no love for us either." She sighed. "Yes, to answer your question. I've known too many who've perished in this endless war. My parents, to offer two examples."

"I'm sorry," Arlo said, lowering his head. "My mother died birthing me, I never knew her."

Zanna reached out, and lifted Arlo's chin with gentle fingers.

"I know," she murmured. "Life is cruel, but there's beauty in it, too."

"The Empire's armies are huge," Arlo muttered, scowling at the apple and changing the subject as the young and curious often do. "You're saying they can't spare a few extra Sparkers and soldiers for us? There must be less than a hundred people up here."

Zanna chuckled. She remembered discussing the same questions with Protector Garet, Solitude's leader, many times.

"There's two hundred. You've not found every nook and cranny of Solitude yet. I'm not sure *I* have. The place is huge. After the monstrous elves, Haltveldt's priority is protecting our shores from the nations overseas, who, as the Emperor would tell us, are just waiting for any sign of weakness. Some might say he's paranoid. Others would say he's a warmonger. Whoever is up here is either old like Severen over there..." She pointed at a grey-bearded old man slumped in a chair against a wall, hands resting on his heaving stomach as he snored. "...or exiled like me."

"Why were you exiled?" Arlo asked, bright eyes fixed on the apple.

"Never you mind," Zanna replied, looking between the boy and the object of his fascination. "What are you doing with that fruit?"

The apple withered. A slow rot spread through it, the green turning brown, then black.

"Stop!" Zanna cried.

She opened her Second Sight, a Sparker's way of seeing the energy of the world. She saw the luminous, green thread running from the apple to Arlo, a black glow flowing in the other direction. She reached out and severed it. The boy jerked backwards, falling off his stool.

"What did you do that for?" he yelled. The other Sparkers turned and watched the commotion, eyebrows raised.

With colour rising in her cheeks, Zanna helped her apprentice back into his seat.

"Arlo, that magic is dangerous. Look at the apple!" The fruit had turned to black mush, its rotten smell overpowering the scent of food and drink around them. "You took too much of its energy and tipped the balance. You can't go around doing that because you feel like it. We have a word for that: Evisceration. And it's *forbidden*, even in battle."

Arlo's eyes were wide. His hands trembled as he gazed at the ruined apple.

"Could a Sparker do that to me?" he asked, voice hushed.

Zanna sighed. She remembered having this same conversation with Calene, twenty years ago. She'd tried to sugar-coat it, and her daughter hadn't appreciated the coddling. It wasn't something she thought she'd discuss with Arlo so soon.

"Yes," she replied, deciding honesty to be the best path this time. "And very few have the strength to shield against it. Raas and Janna forbid us from inflicting this on other humans, even elves, and the Council investigate any who do so."

"Is that the...?"

"The Laws of Engagement, yes. These rules are the reason the people of Haltveldt trust us. We hunt Sparkers who break the Laws and we exterminate them."

Arlo narrowed his eyes, looking between Zanna and the ruined apple.

"You did it, didn't you?" he asked, staring at her without blinking.

This boy is too droking clever.

Zanna nodded. Memories flooded her mind, a face that had haunted her dreams for a decade, and stared at her from the flames. She'd watched it in her mind's eye a thousand times—more—his porcelain skin withering, melting, decaying from the inside out, leaving only a desiccated husk. It thrilled her, as she fed on him, even though something inside her changed. A shadow lurking inside her grew as she Eviscerated him, as she reaved his soul.

She'd never felt so unclean.

"A Sparker attacked me and my daughter. He wanted to take Calene for his own purpose. I had no choice."

"Then why are you here?"

"Some on the Council disagreed and felt I'd overstepped. Including Calene. They sent me to Solitude as a compromise, for services rendered and friends that remained. Lucky for you, they don't mind sending me a Wild Sparker apprentice to tame."

Arlo blew out his cheeks and shook his head. "Your own daughter? I'm sorry, Master. *I* believe you."

Zanna stood and shrugged into her wet cloak. *I'm not sure I do, Arlo,* she thought. *There's always another way.*

"Come on. Let's put some fresh air in our lungs."

The rain and wind had died down a little, but it never truly disappeared from Solitude. Zanna rested against the rampart on the tallest tower, overlooking the Banished lands one hundred feet below, Arlo at her side.

She pulled out her pipe, drew a touch of energy from within herself and channelled it into a small flame on her fingertip, appreciating the gentle warmth as she did. Zanna lit the pipe and inhaled. The talk of her past troubled her, but she found comfort in the still air and the familiar taste of tobacco.

"Smoke?" she asked Arlo, who waved his hands and shook his head in reply.

"Funny, isn't it?" he said. "An exiled person protecting us from the Banished."

"The irony doesn't escape me." Zanna blew a smoke ring. "Many of the souls up here are exiled, unwanted, forgotten. Take our leader Garet, for example. And this is between us, Arlo."

He nodded, eyes wide.

"His parents—still alive, which must make them ancient—made sure he received a place of leadership up here. Big scandal but his family's riches ensured whatever happened isn't common knowledge. And they could pass off their son becoming leader of Solitude as a great honour, but we all know the truth. Solitude is convenient, out of the way, and easy to relocate unwanted baggage."

The moon hid behind the highest rise of the Peaks of Eternity. Black clouds hung heavy in the sky. Zanna's senses felt dull. They told her there should still have been rain. A storm with thunder and lightning. Instead, it felt as though the night held its breath.

"Master?" Arlo asked, his voice subdued as he stared out over the walls. "Does the darkness scare you?"

"You get used to it," Zanna replied, putting an arm around his shoulders.

"No, I mean tonight. There's something... odd."

Zanna glanced at him. She felt it too. The night held a strange quality. All too quiet, but a tense quivering underpinned the silence. Feeling eyes on her, she scanned the rampart and saw they were alone. At first, she thought it her imagination, but faint sounds drifted to her. The sound of whispers that lingered at the edge of her hearing.

"You're right, Arlo," she said, gazing across the ramparts.

Lit braziers dotted the walls that ran a half-mile in each direction. She drew their flames inside her, the sensation thrilling her. Arlo's eyes widened at the depth of her power. Zanna kept pulling fire into her, her limbs filling with warmth, heat, power. It made her feel alive, to the point she wanted to keep drawing, to not let go. A struggle every Sparker contended with.

"We need light."

Quivering with energy and almost at her limit, Zanna lifted her hands to the skies and unleashed a fountain of flame across the heavens, lighting up the plains for miles below them.

"Oh, teeth of the gods," she whispered, taking in the sight below before darkness swallowed the flames.

She turned to Arlo. The colour had drained from his face and tears filled his wide, blue eyes. His fingers dug into the stone ramparts as he gripped the wall.

"Raas preserve us. Get Protector Garet. Run. Can you do that?"

Arlo nodded and shot away, leaving Zanna alone. She

looked out over the ramparts again.

The darkness hid them as they spilled over the distant hills. An army marched across the slate plains towards Solitude. Thousands of them. The Banished were coming.

And less than two hundred Sparkers, with a single apprentice, stood in their way.

CHAPTER TWO
A LONG WAY FROM HOME

'A nobleman from Spring Haven ain't happy 'till he's searched every cupboard in an honest man's house, and taken everything he fancies. Then, he'll burn that man's house down with him in it.' - A Colton trader's view on those from Haltveldt's capital.

"Look," Calene said, thrusting a finger at the rat-faced innkeeper. "I'm caked in filth, I fought droking elves all day yesterday so you could go about your life happy and oblivious to the horrors of war, and I've been travelling for hours through the Forest of droking Mists. Did I mention my head's pounding? I think my brain's about to escape my skull. I'm *bone* tired. Can I at least get changed *before* you give me *more* problems, for Raas' sake?"

The innkeeper shook his head, folding his thin arms across his chest. "Rules are rules. Free board for Sparkers, so long as they serve a citizen's need. So says the Council of Sparkers *and* the Conclave. And I don't appreciate you taking one of the gods' names in vain."

Calene ground her teeth. She glanced over her shoulder. Vettigan, her companion and fellow Sparker, shrugged and sat by the fire. Despite the occasional difference in opinion, the old man remained her closest ally.

Thanks for the help, Calene thought, directing the words into Vettigan's mind with their Link.

Sparkers with a deep connection could connect that way, no matter the distance. It needed a high degree of trust, and the courage to be vulnerable and let someone in. Other than Vettigan, Calene had established the link with one other person. Her mother.

She pushed *that* thought away.

You've got this under control, Vettigan sent back. *You're younger than me, I require immediate warmth.*

He winked as he sank further into his cushioned chair, then closed his eyes and appeared to fall asleep.

Calene turned back to the innkeeper of *The Stubborn Mule*—the only tavern in the whole of Seke Village—and wondered if they'd named the place after him. Maybe he thought he had to live up to the title for appearance's sake. She stared into his pale blue eyes and forced a smile. The innkeeper flinched. She suppressed the urge to roll her eyes.

Why do folk droking react like that? Raas, give me strength!

It's because your 'grin' resembles a lioness baring her teeth, Vettigan projected. *And folk of the Colton Duchy remember all too well the pain of Haltveldt absorbing them. They don't like us.*

Drok off, Calene replied, blocking the Link and taking a deep breath.

"What's your name, friend?" she asked the innkeeper.

"Mannon," he replied, his voice a nasal whine.

Never trust a thin innkeeper, Calene thought.

"Mannon," she said, spreading her hands. "Your little problem in the cellar ain't going anywhere, is it? Let me and my partner over there get settled, stuff some food and drink in our bellies. I *promise* we'll look at the basement tonight. Us Sparkers need to recharge our magic. We'd be useless without a little nourishment, savvy?"

That wasn't true. Sparkers *could* burn out if they exceeded their limits, but so long as they were mindful and had external energies to pull from, the magic flowed. The innkeeper wouldn't know that. The Order of Sparkers weren't ones to divulge their secrets.

"Fine," Mannon said. "Room, food, and one drink each. Then you go down to the basement. After that, you can drink and eat till morning for all I care."

"Great," Calene said, extending her hand. Mannon eyed it before taking it in a slack grip for less than a beat of his shrivelled, little heart, like he thought her fingers would spit venom. "What's the problem down there, anyway?"

"Weird noises," Mannon replied, narrowing his eyes. "Started a few days ago. We don't go down there. It floods so I don't use it."

"Just a wild animal that's got itself trapped, then." Calene took the key Mannon offered. "And my friend's room?"

"You're sharing," Mannon said, with a grin that exposed the gaps between his rotted teeth. "All I can spare."

"Teeth of the gods," Calene muttered, stalking over to Vettigan, snoring by the fire. She kicked his shins and he woke with a start.

"Come on," she said. "Our chamber awaits."

◇

Sitting by the fire, in clean clothes and a cup of red wine in her hand, Calene's mood had improved. Her stomach protested the lack of food, but she could deal with that a while longer.

Other patrons occupied surrounding seats and tables, but it wasn't busy. Most drank alone or made a mess with their food, while a rowdy game of dice played out in the far corner. Smoke hung in the air as men and women enjoyed their pipes. On a stage opposite the fire, a handsome, red-haired man tuned a lute. Mannon hurried him, no doubt eager for something to mask the occasional moan drifting up from below the floor.

Every customer of *The Stubborn Mule* had stolen a glance at Calene and Vettigan, in their bright orange Sparker robes, at least once.

"You wouldn't think a war rages twelve miles from here," Calene muttered, throwing a dark glance around the inn.

Vettigan stared into the flames, the memory of a smile on his lips. They made an odd pair, opposites in almost every way. She'd inherited her darker skin from her mother, but she'd cut her hair short, even shaved it on one side, and dyed the rest blue, to keep from seeing Zanna in the mirror. Combined with sharp and wary eyes, she looked the part of a Sparker and a warrior, through and through. Vettigan's curling, silver hair fell about his face, tangled with his overgrown beard. The robes he wore were at least a size too large. His appearance meant other Sparkers often underestimated him. A mistake. His eyes held the wisdom of an extended life—Vettigan would turn one hundred and eight on his next name day, though he appeared no older than sixty. A Sparker's fortune.

Calene had known him all her life and he'd taken her under his wing after her mother's exile. They weren't master and apprentice but allies; Calene had the greater power and skill, Vettigan a vast well of knowledge.

"What does it matter to these simple folk?" Vettigan replied, sweeping his gaze across the inn, laughing when the lute player strummed the jaunty first chords of *A Maid Goes to Spring Haven*. "The capital may as well be on another continent for all the patrons of *The Stubborn Mule* care. They're odd people in this part of the world, allied themselves with the elves for centuries. Remember that statue we happened by, towering into the sky? An elven figure, yet the humans here prayed to it like Sparkers petitioning Raas or Janna."

"Not a lot of Sparkers petitioning Raas and Janna these days," Calene said.

Vettigan took a pull from his tankard, a faraway look in his eye.

"Maybe the elven gods walked the earth like ours once did," he said. "Maybe they still would if we weren't killing them all."

"It makes you sad, doesn't it?" Calene muttered. "The war."

"Many things sadden me, Calene. Changes in Haltveldt have gathered pace this last decade since Locke ascended the throne, and not many for the better. The rulers of Haltveldt have battled elves for centuries, longer some say. Murdered, enslaved or segregated them. They slaughter every elven child they find with the Spark. It's a gift, Calene. To destroy it like that... It goes against the gods."

"Vettigan, anything you dislike 'goes against the gods.'" Her words carried no heat. These days, she found it hard to disagree with her friend's complaints against Haltveldt.

Vettigan let out a heavy sigh. "They'll drive them to extinction—or throw them into the slums to join the other slaves. And then what? Who will be left for the mighty Empire to make war with?"

She nodded. "All the duchies have fallen in line. There's no one left on this continent to fight against. Hard to believe the Empire rose from a single city."

"Every tree springs from a seed. But Spring Haven proved a rotten one... After the elves, they'll find a new enemy ripe for conquest. Mark my words, Calene."

Calene patted his hand. She understood. The war with the elves seemed pointless to her. They'd spent the last three months on duty at the front, protecting soldiers and fighting wherever the Laws of Engagement permitted, the latest tour in a long line. Every time they were cycled out, she felt relief.

Few shared the Council and the Emperor of Haltveldt's thirst for war, but what the Council decreed, the Sparkers carried out. Since the Emperor had appointed his friend Balz as High Sparker, the orders were executed without question. Raas decreed that those with the Spark should serve and, for the most part, the magi did their duty.

"Tranquil here, so far from Spring Haven, isn't it?" Calene murmured, glancing around at the inn's patrons, drinking and carousing without a care in the world. "Even with a war on their doorstep."

Only the peace couldn't take root in her. Her thoughts drifted to her father and, when she forced them away, snarling, her mother's image appeared in her mind instead.

Calene wondered if she warmed herself by a fire in Solitude, knitting in silence with the rest of the world so far away. She rejected that thought too, digging her fingernails into the palms of her hands until she felt pain, anger. Not the inklings of longing.

She deserves her banishment, Calene told herself, biting her tongue for good measure.

"You should talk to her," Vettigan muttered, watching her over the rim of his ale. Even with their Link blocked, he knew where her mind had strayed.

"No," she replied, looking away. "I'm not having this conversation again."

"A decade has passed. You should forgive Zanna. She acted on impulse, a mother's instinct. Don't you think she's suffered enough?"

That night flashed in Calene's mind, when her mother had Eviscerated another living soul. Her father had taken a black path, became one of those Sparkers who'd rejected Raas' decree and believed Sparkers should dominate. In the last ten years, Calene's nightmares had alternated between visions of what her father planned to do with her, and his skin and bones withering and melting, forming an ooze that stained the floor of their home.

"There's always another way." She flicked a tear from her eye. "What she did was unforgivable. She's lucky they only exiled her."

"Exile, pah! A farce and you know it," Vettigan said. "I'd have done the same in her shoes."

"I know," Calene replied, "and that's why I don't want to talk about it."

They fell silent as Mannon delivered a tray laden with cheese, bread, stew and olives. Calene's stomach rumbled with such fierceness the innkeeper did a double-take. Colour rose in her cheeks as she tucked in, tearing off a chunk of bread to dip into her beef stew.

"Eat with haste," Mannon said, placing a jug of water down on the table with a thump. "I don't want whatever is in my cellar there any longer. Bad for business."

Calene rolled her eyes. Neither Sparker spoke as they shovelled food into their mouths. They'd spent vast amounts of energy protecting and fortifying Haltveldt's soldiers and warding off spells from the elven mages. They were fewer in number these days, but they didn't share the same limits as human Sparkers. The elves in the city—listless slaves severed from magic—seemed alien to their free brethren.

The free elves fought for their lives. No Laws of Engagement, no decree of the gods, no Council to regulate their magic. And they didn't pull their punches in battle. Calene shuddered at the thought of the Sparkers who'd let their shields slip, their withered faces as they turned to mush lingering at the edges of her mind.

For years, the Council, compelled by the various Emperors of Haltveldt, had exploited loopholes to force Sparkers into being more proactive in battle. Why give a Sparker a sword when they could wield the elements? Calene had seen war. She understood the push to relax, or even abolish, the Laws. It would bring an end to the conflict sooner.

She feared Vettigan's words were correct; the elven race would become nothing more than a sad memory and Haltveldt would find a new enemy to obliterate.

"Getting thirsty," Vettigan grunted, showing Calene his empty tankard.

"Aye," she replied, draining her wine. "An evening of drinking is just what's needed. Let's get this sorted."

———◆———

Mannon inserted the key into the brass lock and dust

exploded from the door frame as he barged it open with his shoulder. The hinges creaked from lack of use.

"When did you last hear the moans?" Calene coughed, wiping dust off her skin.

"You heard them as you drank," the innkeeper grunted, backing away from the cellar's entrance. "They stop when the music plays."

"A spectre?" Vettigan asked, drawing the flame from a nearby candle and holding it in his palm. "Any deaths here of late?"

"Nothing recent." Mannon held a gaunt hand over his mouth and spoke through his fingers, like he feared the patrons upstairs would overhear. "Are you saying my inn's haunted?"

"Just discussing options," Calene said, throwing Vettigan a baleful stare. He shrugged. "Go see to your guests, innkeeper. Whatever it is, it won't keep us long."

"Just don't cause any mayhem," Mannon said, eyeing the fire in Vettigan's palm. "Most of this place is wood."

The innkeeper slinked off, muttering to himself. Calene thought she caught the words *teeth* and *gods*.

"*Spectres*?" she asked, grinning at the other Sparker. "Did you have to tease him?"

"You never know," Vettigan chuckled, "though more likely it's a dog swept in by the flooding. The jobs we do for a full belly."

"Maybe a merperson, then. They enjoy the water." Calene winked. "After you?"

Vettigan stepped forward, his fire illuminating the

brick steps that descended into the cellar. The stink of damp rot filled Calene's nostrils as she listened to her friend's footsteps echo around the winding stairs. The bard's music drifted from above, and Calene reckoned they were below the stage area.

"Wait," Vettigan whispered.

Goosebumps swept over Calene's skin. Vettigan had opened his Second Sight, checking to make sure nothing magical dwelled in the cellar. Calene's senses only picked up on it because they were so attuned to him. Vettigan wielded his abilities like a needle where other Sparkers beat away at their problems with a warhammer. In the gloom, she saw him turn her way, and press a fingertip to his temple. Calene unblocked their Link.

I sense a heartbeat, far side of the cellar. It's weak. No Spark. Definitely not a dog.

A sensation itched in a separate corner of Calene's mind—the part reserved for communication with her mother. Zanna hadn't attempted to Link with her for over five years. Calene had made it clear then that she shouldn't try again.

Since, Calene had trained her mind to keep the barriers blocking communication with her mother strong. She ignored the itch.

The moaning tells me it's injured or dying, Calene projected. *I'll try talking first.*

She moved past Vettigan and stood at the edge of the firelight. Listening, she heard the slow drip of water against the stone floor and the shallow rattle of something close to its last breath.

"Hello?" she called. "We're here to help you."

Heartbeat increasing, Vettigan projected.

A soft moan answered, then turned into a hacking cough. Calene pinpointed its origin.

"Come on," she said.

She trotted across the abandoned cellar, heading towards the dripping water. Mannon claimed he'd heard the cries start a few days before. The thing trapped in the basement had dragged itself next to the water—the only source of nourishment they could get.

As Vettigan's fire illuminated the cellar's far side, Calene stopped with a gasp. "Raas and the rotten teeth of the gods."

A white-haired, pale man with yellow eyes lay on the floor, staring up at the ceiling as the bard's music continued to drift down. The figure wore fur clothing, with daggers of varying sizes tucked into a belt around his waist. A broadsword lay discarded on the floor. The smell of vomit, excrement and urine assaulted Calene's nose and made her gag. She glanced at Vettigan, who covered his nose and mouth with his sleeve. One of the man's legs bent at an odd angle, and lacerations caked with dried blood covered his visible skin.

"How is he still alive?" she muttered.

Calene took another step forward and crouched, drawing on her own energy to send out a sliver of air magic, pushing away the stench. The man on the floor flopped his head to the side, staring at her with squinted eyes, as though the firelight hurt them. He didn't seem to have the strength to lift his hand and shield them.

"He's listening to the music," Vettigan said, drawing alongside Calene, eyes wide. "That's why the moans stop. The sound comforts him."

"What is he?" Calene asked.

She studied the stranger. She'd thought him pale before, but now she saw his skin to be white as chalk, as though it lacked pigment. He worked his mouth, trying to speak. Calene drew on the water from the cellar and cupped her hands. Liquid pooled between them. She held them out and nodded. The stranger opened his mouth and she trickled the water between his grey lips.

"Calene," Vettigan murmured, pointing at the broadsword. "Look at the design on the crossguard. Does it look familiar to you?"

She tore her eyes away from the stranger and glanced at the weapon. A bronze emblem stood out at the centre of the crossguard: the image of a gigantic fortress, battlements behind it, and a sun high in the sky above the ramparts.

"Solitude," she whispered. "From the far side. I remember visiting as a girl. Mother took me beyond the gates."

"Yes," Vettigan said. "If I'm not mistaken, our pale friend is one of the Banished. Council tells us to exterminate any this side of Solitude on sight—not that we've ever had to—but that won't tell us how it appeared here. Look at his sword. He doesn't look a simple shepherd, does he?"

"Is... as... dorachas Solitude's... em," the Banished croaked, the sound like old parchment tearing.

The itch in Calene's mind grew into an incessant pounding. Her mother wasn't giving up. She bit her lip.

"I'm not letting him die," she said. "Shove the rules. I've killed too many in my life but at least they were trying to kill me. He's helpless. I want to at least talk to this one first, if I can."

Vettigan nodded and got to his feet, holding his flame closer to the wall and running his hand over it. He pulled it away, showing Calene the soot on his fingers.

"Look," he said. "Burn marks on the wall. Days old, but no sign of fire anywhere else."

Calene looked into the Banished's eyes. Despite his weaponry, he appeared gentle. He smiled back at her. He lifted a trembling hand and pointed at the ceiling.

"Go bheaut," he whispered, then his hand flopped back to the floor. His eyes fell closed.

"Drok the rules," Calene said.

She opened her senses and drew on the energies she could reach—fire, water, earth, the raw emotions of joy, frustration and contentment from upstairs. She pulled them all into herself, letting the exhilaration of life run through her. The stench from the wounded man thicker in her nose, her eyesight sharper, her heart beating with more strength and speed as her Spark made her *more*. Calene placed her hands on the Banished's forehead.

"Sorry, friend. This will hurt."

With a jolt, she flooded the dying man with the energy coursing through her body, a small bubble of reluctance rising in Calene's stomach as she did. When she fed her

Spark, she often wanted to keep it all for herself. A Spark-er's curse.

The injured man's eyes flew open and his back arched as he let out a high-pitched scream. Calene pulled her hands away and sat back panting. The Banished slumped to the ground, eyes again closed.

"He's breathing," Vettigan murmured, picking up the sword and giving it a swing. "Good blade, well-balanced. If he's a farmer or a shepherd, I'm the Emperor's nanny."

As Calene opened her mouth to answer, the walls of her mind separating her from her mother crumbled. Like a burst dam unleashed, memories of times they'd shared, held behind the unblemished obsidian barriers blocking the Link, flooded her mind. Calene falling, grazing her knee, her mother's smiling face as she used the Spark to heal it; Zanna beaming with pride as Calene produced flames for the first time; staying up to watch the sunset as they spoke about the gods' ways and their magic. The soul-deep relief Calene felt when she awoke on her father's slab, alive, to see Zanna had rescued her. The crushing despair she felt when she saw the remains of the man, and her mother, tears staining her face, standing over him.

Love, warmth, regret, pity, anger, self-loathing, pride—so many emotions, too many to process and name—washed through her brain. Calene fell backwards, head smacking against the stone floor.

Calene, I'm sorry but I had to reach you. The Banished... they're at Solitude's gates. Thousands and more yet arriving. You must get word to the Council. Please.

Calene raised a shaking hand to her forehead as she pushed herself up. She stared at the sleeping Banished she'd healed, stomach churning, vision spinning. Grunting, she exerted any will she could muster on the emotions swirling inside her. Steady, she focused on the Link.

Mother, she replied, feeling a wave of relief and gratitude flooding back along their connection. *There's one lying right in front of me, and I just saved his life.*

CHAPTER THREE
THE POLITICS OF WAR

'If someone from Haltveldt tells me the dish is meatballs and pasta, I'll check under the sauce to make sure.' - A successful Octarian sailor holds a healthy amount of distrust for those from Haltveldt.

"Raas preserve us. Janna too, for that matter."

Kade examined his reflection in the mirror. To his eyes, he'd aged in the two hours since the carrier pigeon had arrived from Solitude. He splashed water over his tan skin, rubbing with vigour at the frown lines on his forehead. Kade knew he could descend into the depths of vanity all too often, but he needed to look his best when he presented Solitude's case to the Conclave of Spring Haven and the Council of Sparkers.

Kade tired of Haltveldt's politics. Just when he thought he'd appeased the Conclave, the Sparkers would rear their magical heads. Often, it had felt like they did it just to be contrary.

Things had changed since Balz's rise. Now, the Conclave and Council acted as one. That unsettled him even more.

All too often, Kade felt overlooked—a junior Master, his sole duty liaising with a Sparker stronghold. Many viewed his role as a joke.

Liaison to Solitude, Kade thought with a grimace. *Fancy way of saying babysitter to a group of forgotten old men and women, standing watch over a near-extinct race of shepherds.*

Emperor Locke sat in on all meetings of state and took a keen interest in those involving war. His thirst for blood surpassed even his father's, and he cared not a fig for Kade or his thoughts. He wondered if the Emperor knew where Solitude lay on a map.

Maybe the prospect of a battle would sway the Emperor into committing an army to bolster against the Banished's sudden mustering, but he'd need a majority in the Conclave to lend support first. He couldn't begin to comprehend the whims of Haltveldt's sovereign.

He eyed the thin strip of paper again, one of several sent with an identical message in case one bird didn't complete the journey to Spring Haven.

Kade. Banished have flooded Solitude's plains. Thousands more pour over the hills. We number less than two hundred; old, burned out or worse. We NEED an army. Do what you must, but with haste.

Garet

Solitude lay eight hundred miles north-east of Spring Haven; it'd taken the birds a full day to reach their destination. Kade sent a reply, assuring he'd ask for aid. He cursed the lack of immediate communication. The Sparkers stationed at Solitude were old, forgotten loners; any they'd shared a Link with were dead, or had severed ties. The giant fortress wasn't a place for Haltveldt's popular and brightest.

True, Zanna Alpenwood, the exile, had a contact in Haltveldt she could Link with, but half the Council didn't trust her.

No dice, anyway, Kade thought. Zanna's daughter wouldn't return to Spring Haven for weeks. Kade ground his teeth.

Every Sparker in Solitude could be dead already. Including Arlo.

Think positive, Kade thought, running a hand through his raven-coloured hair. *Zanna will keep him safe. The further he is from the vultures in Spring Haven, the better.*

Old doubts bubbled to the surface of Kade's mind, but he rejected them. Sending his son to Solitude had made sense for them both. What chance did he have of protecting his son from the Emperor's dogs?

But Zanna? Even in exile, her talent remained unmatched. He knew why she lived in disgrace and he saw it for what it was—a mother's love. He could trust her to protect Arlo, even knowing his heritage. She would keep their secret safe. Arlo's bloodline had become too obvious now for her not to notice, yet she offered only reassurances in her letters.

Without thinking, Kade's fingers grazed the chain he wore around his neck. Arlo's mother had given it to him, a lifetime ago—or so it felt. It hadn't been a typical

Haltveldtian wedding—midnight vows and a sympathetic
Sparker, an old friend of the family, to conduct the cere-
mony. The man had fallen in battle soon after, taking the
secret to his grave. Men like the Emperor had forced that
secrecy on them and, to that day, he hated them in ways he
never spoke aloud.

Twelve years, she'd been gone. He had never stopped
missing her. She'd lived just long enough to bring their
son into the world. Kade had found himself a widower at
twenty-two with a new-born.

He'd always thanked the gods that Arlo had inherited his mother's looks; a gift so Kade would never forget
her face, though he recognised the curse in the favour.
One day, the boy's elven features would become too pro-
nounced to conceal. He'd prayed to Raas often, begging
for fortune so his son would remain safe at his side. Then,
the boy Sparked, and forced Kade's hand.

If he'd apprenticed at the University, like most Sparkers, his heritage would soon have been discovered and
they'd all have paid the price for Kade's past.

Though his apartment granted him privacy, Kade still
glanced around before drawing the small box of Octarian
spice from his dresser. He held it to his nose and sniffed.
The dust punched away his tiredness and cleared his mind
in a heartbeat.

"As soon as we deal with the Banished," Kade said, to
the snuffbox, "I'm giving you up."

He grimaced as soon as the words left his mouth.
How many times had he said that before? How many
times that day?

Returning the spice to the drawer and slamming it shut, he strapped his sword-belt and scabbard to his hip and strode from his chambers.

Like most members of the Emperor's Conclave, Kade lived near Haltveldt Keep, though the position he held granted him little favour or power. Kade thanked the gods the news from Solitude had arrived *before* a scheduled meeting; he'd have little chance of calling one himself.

Haltveldt Keep dominated Spring Haven; situated in its dead centre, only the Sparker's University rivalled it in grandeur. Built to withstand siege for decades, the city had grown around it, mirroring the nation of Haltveldt's slow march across the continent over the last two thousand years. The elven nation was the last to withstand the Empire, and Kade believed they'd surrender before long. Or they'd face genocide.

He hoped they'd avoid either fate. For the elves, surrender meant slavery and, for those with the Spark, execution.

Kade strode through the marble halls, head down and lost in thought. People in the capital paid Solitude little heed—the Banished were terrors to scare children, little more than simple shepherds to the masses—but their return in such great numbers *had* to change the Emperor's mind.

Though, with the snakes surrounding him, it's tough to

call, Kade thought, as he arrived at the Conclave's meeting hall.

A gigantic square table took up most of the chamber, dominated by a gaudy, oversized, gilded chair in the middle of one side. An additional forty-eight smaller seats surrounded it. Around the room, statues of heroes from Haltveldt's past looked down with solemn faces. Kade gazed up at the warrior, Byar; enshrined in legend as the one who'd led the charge against the Banished, then protected Spring Haven when the alliance between duchies broke down and the elves plotted against humankind.

Or so we're told, Kade mused, his mouth twisting as he studied Byar's stone face. *He always looked too cruel for my liking.*

First to arrive, Kade took his place on the opposite side of the table to the Emperor's seat. Many of the Masters would jostle for seats near the Emperor's own, but those with a little more cunning would place themselves where they could catch his eye and study his mood. He knew Bertrand, the Master of Ceremonies—an excellent friend—would sit opposite the Emperor, too. Bertrand received requests to speak from the Masters, and the urgency of Kade's news couldn't wait. Conclave meetings were battlegrounds of their own, and Kade *had* to make a powerful account of himself for Solitude. For Arlo.

As if summoned, Bertrand rushed into the room. Kade breathed a sigh of relief to see him alone. The Master of Ceremonies gave a casual wave when he laid eyes on him.

"Kade," he said, his ringing voice jovial. "Early? Has Solitude run out of wine?"

Bertrand laughed at his own joke. Kade could count on one hand the number of meetings to which he'd arrived on time, let alone early. Bertrand heaved his massive frame into a chair, chins wobbling as his backside struck the velvet seat. Producing a silk handkerchief, he wiped sweat from his lined brow and patted down the silver curls on his head.

"I have urgent news," Kade said, eyeing more conclave members entering the chambers. "I *must* speak first."

Bertrand laughed again, but the mirth dissipated as Kade's eyes drilled into his.

"You're serious?" he asked, ignoring the greetings from the other arrivals. "Opening a Conclave meeting with matters regarding *Solitude*? Look, trade with Avastia and Octaria's been banned; their ships aren't allowed to dock at our ports. Then there's the never-ending war with the elves, the riots in Protector's Watch. Maybe I can get you a space to address the Conclave towards the end, if there's time."

"No!" Kade growled, slamming his hand on the table. He swallowed, took a deep breath and muzzled his temper. That was the spice talking. "No. I must speak first."

Bertrand's eyes narrowed, but he nodded. "It'd better be worth it, Kade. Though I suppose your stock couldn't fall much lower."

Arlo's smiling face flashed in Kade's mind, bringing memories of the boy's mother. *Oh, my friend,* he thought, *you don't know the half of it.*

"Bertrand!" a deep voice called. "Well met. And Master Kade Besem, how fares Solitude? Any sheep bothering those mighty Sparkers up there?"

Kade looked up. Uriel, Master of Coin, a wizened rake of a man, sauntered toward them, an easy grin on his face. Kade returned it, despite the good-natured barb. He'd known the fellow since childhood. Their family estates bordered one another.

"Uriel, you old dog," Bertrand laughed as they shook hands. "Thought the Emperor's lackeys had asked you to retire?"

"Aye," Uriel said with a shrug. "Problem is, my records are a mess and I'm the only one who can understand them. It'd take years to get them in order."

Kade laughed, despite the sick feeling in his stomach, and watched the Master of Coin take his place close to the Emperor's seat.

"A decent man," he said to Bertrand, who nodded in agreement.

"Too few of those," the Master of Ceremonies muttered. "Speaking of which..."

Two tall, handsome men swept into the chamber. Dressed in black and silver, each wore their golden hair in the same style, beards trimmed, oiled neat. Nexes, the taller, more muscular of the two, held the rank of Master of War and, if rumour proved correct, enjoyed more than just political favour with the Emperor.

The other, Balz, had ascended the ranks of Sparkers with astonishing speed, becoming the youngest High

Sparker in the Council's history. His rise had sent ripples through the whole of Haltveldt; the Emperor had replaced key people in the Conclave, transgressing long-standing alliances and timeworn tradition to place *his* people in the positions that mattered. With Balz in place, the Emperor controlled the Sparkers and everyone knew it. Kade didn't even need to sniff to smell the change in the air.

Nexes, Balz and Emperor Locke were lifelong friends, and a wise man bore that in mind.

Kade looked around for Zal—apprentice Sparker to the old warhorse, Ganton, and close friend of the Emperor's coterie—but he was absent. These days, it wasn't unusual to see him sitting in on Conclave meetings, despite his junior station. The Emperor did as he pleased. Why not today?

Nexes nodded at Bertrand and held up a single finger. The Master of Ceremonies shook his head and held up two in reply. The Master of War's eyebrows shot up in surprise. Then he glanced at Kade and sneered.

"The elven blight will soon be over," he called, cocking his head to one side. "Does this upset you, Kade?"

"Me?" he replied, fighting to keep his expression bland. "Why should I care?"

Nexes smiled back, an icy grin that didn't reach his emerald eyes.

The sound of metal clanging on marble rang out, echoing between the stone statues and marble floors. The Conclave members got to their feet as the Emperor's herald cleared his throat. Kade lent Bertrand a helping hand.

"Locke, first of his name, Emperor of Haltveldt and the Eight Duchies. Favoured by Raas, Lord of Gods, who once walked the Emperor's lands. He who bows to no man."

The Emperor sauntered in, nodding to Masters of the Conclave at random. Short, slight, and with facial features too large for his face, Locke moved with an air of privileged confidence—the walk no other citizen of Haltveldt could dream of pulling off. Arrogant, petulant and pampered, the Emperor possessed a cunning intelligence and physical prowess at odds with his appearance. Ruthlessness ran through the young sovereign's blood. Few believed his father had died of old age.

As the Emperor took his seat, clasping hands with Nexes and Balz who sat either side of him, the Conclave took their seats. Bertrand remained standing.

"Gentlemen," he began, sweeping his gaze across the chamber. Despite his queasiness, Kade felt a smile reach his lips. He enjoyed the Master of Ceremonies' penchant for the theatrical. "Welcome. Emperor Locke, may I extend the Conclave's eternal gratitude. Our first speaker is Master Kade Besem, Liaison to Solitude, who wishes to speak regarding...urgent news from the north, and those brave men and women who guard our beloved continent from the hordes beyond the wall."

This brought sniggers from some and open laughter from Nexes and—Kade noted with a heavy heart—Balz, whose support he depended on as High Sparker. He thrust his shaking hands into his pockets as he stood. The Octarian spice had lost its fire at the wrong time. Swallowing, he gazed at Emperor Locke, who met his stare without expression.

"Emperor Locke, my fellow Masters of the Conclave," he began, voice cracking and shrill in his own ears. He cleared his throat and focused on his task, on the lives up in Solitude. On Arlo. "What do our histories tell us? Of the sacrifices, bloodshed and horror our ancestors suffered as they drove the Banished northwards. Of the toil in building Solitude, brick-by-brick, as they held the horde at bay? A magnificent feat of warcraft, enshrined in the annals of legend as one of our people's greatest moments."

Watching the Emperor, Kade noticed a tick around his eye at those words. At least it showed that the man paid attention.

"They fought a centuries-long battle against that magical horde of enslavers. The sacrifices they made so we might enjoy our freedom are their gift to us. But they are also an obligation. Now, two hundred Sparkers man a stronghold that guards the pass through the Peaks of Eternity into Banished lands. A mere two hundred."

"I didn't realise you taught history, Master Besem," Balz jeered, spreading his hands. "I suppose you've nothing better to do."

The members of the Conclave laughed. The Emperor smiled—it didn't reach his shrewd, cold eyes—and nodded at Kade to continue.

"This morning, I received word. The plains of Solitude are brimming with Banished, and more follow. This can mean only one thing. Invasion."

Cries erupted from the Conclave. The Emperor and his friends sat still, staring at Kade, ignoring the shouts from the rest of the table. Bertrand rose to his feet, arms wide.

"Silence!" he yelled, his powerful voice piercing the cacophony. The Masters obeyed. "Continue, Master Kade."

"Emperor Locke, Master of War Nexes, High Sparker Balz. I beseech you; send an army with Sparkers to Solitude's aid. We cannot let it fall. For our ancestors' sake. For the sake of all Haltveldt."

And for my son.

Silence filled the room. Bertrand tugged at Kade's sleeve, reminding him to sit. As he did, Nexes rose.

"The Banished. A terrible threat." He swept his gaze across the Conclave. Hope bloomed in Kade's chest. Nexes appeared focused, serious. "High Sparker Balz, have you received word from Solitude confirming this?"

Balz, considering his fingernails, flicked his eyes to Kade then back.

"No."

"Odd. One might have thought they'd send word to you, of all people. What say you, Master Tellem? As Master of Trade, you have connections far and wide. You of all people *must* have heard whispers?"

Kade stared at Tellem. A weasel in more than just looks, the greasy little man flashed his rodent teeth before bowing his head to Nexes. "No, Master of War. Of

Solitude, I've heard not a peep. Not for months, in fact. Adhraas is only ten mile south, right on the fortress's doorstep, but still... Not a peep. Sea's Keep, now, they're reporting growing numbers of Avastian ships on their horizon."

"Avastian, you say? A credible threat, which is why trade with those pirates is closed. Anyone else?" Nexes folded his arms across his chest and waited. Silence answered. Nodding, his gaze returned to Balz. "What do you make of our good liaison's news, High Sparker? It appears only he's aware of this...horde of Banished."

"I believe someone is looking to embarrass the fellow," Balz said, stifling a yawn, "or Master Besem's imagination has gotten the better of him. The Banished are simple folk now, rustic and few. Bogeymen to scare children and old men. As Master Tellem warns, there are real threats out there. Elves, Avastians, Octarians—they watch our mighty empire for any sign of weakness. Sending our armies north on a wild goose chase, giving the elves respite, is what our enemies are waiting for."

Nexes smiled, before settling a withering stare on Kade.

"There you have it. Of course, I have my own theories on why Master Kade would wish to split our armies from war with the elves... Old *attachments* die hard, don't they, my friend? You shame yourself with your transparent ploy to increase your worth, Kade. Just when I believed your stock couldn't sink any further."

Arguments died on Kade's lips. The stares of the conclave lingered on him as his blood turned to ice; speculating minds and unheard whispers pressed down on him. The spice had well and truly left him.

"There's an elven army on our doorstep to the south. Nations overseas wait for us to falter. You want Haltveldt to fail? Now? When we have so much more to achieve? So much within our reach? We must project *strength* to our many enemies, not jump at shadows. Do you have anything more to add, Kade? Or shall we put this sorry matter to rest, and you can crawl back into your snuffbox?"

Kade lowered his eyes to the table, ignoring the barb. Everyone knew about his spice addiction. Instead, the other threat hooked him. *Attachments die hard… He can't know about Arlo's mother. How could he? How could anyone?*

"No, Master Nexes."

"Excellent," the Master of War replied. "To important matters then. High Sparker Balz tells me more Sparkers and Haltveldt soldiers are slaughtered by the day because our elven foes embrace magic we have erroneously forbidden. The Laws of Engagement are out-dated. Some old Master, centuries ago in a time of peace, claimed he happened upon words from Raas himself, and designed to shackle our Sparkers. Because of these *unverified* divine instructions, we struggle to wage a war on an uneven footing. We've tried, believe me. We've sought to push past these tired, dogmatic laws but they hinder our true potential. Without the Laws, we'd have dealt with the elven threat decades ago. Our Emperor, I have seen the light; I've prayed and sought counsel from High Sparker Balz and he has assured me of the truth. Our gods wouldn't see us slaughtered, wouldn't see us struggle impotently while innocents die by the thousands."

"No..." Kade whispered, returning his gaze to Nexes. The man's eyes fixed on him.

"As my wartime powers decree, I request an immediate vote to remove the Laws of Engagement from our Sparkers. Let them fight to the fullest of their abilities with the power of Evisceration. Let us defeat the elven scourge, once and for all, then prepare to move with full strength against our next foes. "

"Raas and Janna themselves set the Laws of Engagement," Uriel grated. "How dare you even *suggest* abandoning them?"

Others agreed, slamming fists on the Conclave table, shouting to the vaulted ceilings so their voices would be heard. Kade shook his head; he knew which way this vote would go.

"The gods' Laws!" someone cried. "Blasphemy!"

"The Laws set the Sparkers apart from tyrants!" another yelled. "We'd lose the trust of the people in an instant!"

"Allow Sparkers to run unchecked? Madness!"

Those protesting Nexes' words didn't shock Kade. They were the older council members, those too unimportant to replace or the ones Emperor Locke hadn't yet uprooted. His people, the Conclave members belonging to him, remained silent. Except Tellem.

"The people will believe what we tell them, as it's ever

been," the Master of Trade snarled. "You want more of our soldiers to die at the hands of the elven filth? More of our Sparkers turned to mush? Fools!"

The Emperor held up a hand. Nexes took his seat and gazed across at Kade, as the voices dwindled to a murmur, then fell silent.

"Who made the Laws of Engagement?" the Emperor asked. "The gods? Or meddling old men with nothing better to do, high on their own sense of importance? Give me definitive proof of the former, please. Anyone?" He waited. "No, I thought not. A vote then. Hands will do. Bertrand, my loyal Master of Ceremonies? Count them. All for."

The Emperor kept his hand raised. One-by-one, the other Conclave members followed him. Kade, fists bunched by his sides, studied the faces of those agreeing, some with shame etched into their features but many more smiling in victory. A defiant handful, himself and Uriel included, kept their hands down. And marked their cards in the process.

Emperor Locke swept his gaze around the table, winking at Nexes, then settled on High Sparker Balz. "I hereby repeal the Laws of Engagement, and allow use of all Spark magic in battle, up to and including Evisceration. A momentous occasion, I think we can all agree. No more business for today."

The Emperor moved to his feet as shouts rang out around the chamber once more. Uriel's face turned purple as spittle flew from his lips. Balz and Nexes followed. Kade leaned back in his chair, stunned. The Laws kept Sparkers on the side of good and made the citizens of Haltveldt believe the Order would protect them. Without them...

A tap on his shoulder made Kade glance around. Nexes crouched behind him, mouth to his ear.

"The sub-human scum will get what they deserve, elf-lover, and so will anyone who sympathises with them. Mark my words. You made a fatal mistake today."

He knows, Kade thought. *Drok! He knows. How?*

He remained seated as the Conclave chamber emptied. Bertrand stayed at his side, shaking his head as he stared at the Emperor's now-vacant chair.

"My Empire is dead," he murmured, as the last Masters filed from the room. "The killing won't end with the elves. Haltveldt is too fond of war. Who's next for the slaughter?"

"Solitude," Kade replied, thinking of his son. "They're defenceless, and the threat is real. I know it! We can't let that happen, Bertrand. We must move with haste."

CHAPTER FOUR
LESSONS FROM THE PAST

'They say Solitude has stood for 2,000 years, or thereabouts. Utter drok. Its bones are more ancient than that, and if the men of Spring Haven built it, I'm from Velen.' - From the Journals of Matrim the Mad.

Zanna stood on Solitude's highest rampart, her dark purple hood pulled up to keep off the hammering rain, and watched the Banished horde below.

Two days had passed since the vanguard arrived, and the flow of bodies descending from the shale-filled foothills had slowed to a trickle. By the amount of campfires dotting the plains each night, the Sparkers estimated the number of Banished exceeded four hundred thousand. Garet had sent birds to Spring Haven, warning of imminent invasion.

Yet the Banished hadn't attacked.

"Afraid of our magic," some of the other Sparkers insisted. Zanna wasn't so sure.

Caravans filled with women and children moved

behind the vanguard. Armies didn't bring their families to war. Then came her Link with Calene, and news of her discovery. The Banished male she'd stumbled upon, so far from home—a mystery Zanna felt certain they had to solve, and with haste.

She probed her Link to Calene, basking for a moment in the comfort of sharing a piece of herself with her daughter again. It felt like a passage had reopened, bringing warmth and light where before there had been only cold and darkness for so long. Like a flower, she basked in that glow. So far, their communication remained curt and professional but it didn't curdle her joy. Zanna sensed Calene's resentment, her lingering judgement, but hoped their forced reconnection could become the catalyst for reconciliation.

A fool's hope, perhaps, but a mother's hope.

A wave of agitation ran through the Banished. *This isn't an invasion,* Zanna thought, tapping her lips. *It's a migration.*

"I wish they'd attack," Garet grumbled. Zanna gave a start; she'd forgotten the Protector stood there, at her side, projecting a shield of air to keep the rain off him.

One hundred and seventy years old, the man stood tall and swarthy; neither fat nor thin, but thick. A bitter twist marred noble features, framed by curled, raven hair. Dyed, Zanna reckoned. Standing beside him, she felt his power and considered his reputation. Garet's Spark outstripped most living magicians, though rumours of illicit experiments had caused his banishment a century before.

Only his family connections had saved him from execution.

Solitude's decline had sped up on his watch. He didn't disdain the place, as others did. He seemed to genuinely care for his role as Protector. But he lacked the skills necessary to lead. Impatience steered him, like he longed for battle. Often, Zanna found him poring over reports from the elven front, his face eager as he drank in the details. Now, at last, war had found him.

Standing near him brought thoughts of her husband unbidden to her mind. Zanna suppressed a shudder.

"It's infuriating, all this needless waiting," Garet grumbled, glaring daggers down at the plains. His ice-blue eyes flashed in the cold light. "I wish they'd make a move so we can fight back. Damn the Laws!"

Zanna shook her head. She made it her policy to stay out of Garet's way, and he seemed to prefer it that way. Her Spark outstripped his, and he didn't enjoy feeling inferior to anyone.

"The Laws hold meaning. Without them, Sparkers become tyrants. It's the will of the gods. The Spark is their gift to us, and we must follow their commands. Or did you forget we're a religious order first, and the Emperor's dogs of war second?"

"Mind yourself," Garet warned. "We're a long way from Spring Haven but the Emperor has ears everywhere. The Laws are out-dated; without them, you and I would live free." He scoffed. "Who's to say the gods ever existed anyway? Have you met them? No. Normal folk require betters to lead them—and who better than us?"

"What would you do, Garet, if the Laws didn't exist?" Zanna asked, pointing towards the Banished. Music drifted to her from below—strings, wind instruments and voices raised in song, a language she didn't understand—a beautiful melody unlike any she'd heard before.

"I would rain fire upon their heads; rend the earth beneath them." He nodded to himself. "And if they reached our walls, I would Eviscerate them, so that any who fled would remember what happened the day they challenged the might of Solitude."

"They haven't attacked us," Zanna said, a wave of contempt flooding through her.

Evisceration? He'd go that far? Yes, I suppose he would. And others would follow. The Laws were meant for men like Garet.

"Yet." Garet replied. "Better to be safe."

"And that," Zanna said, turning to face the Protector, her face like stone, "is why we need the gods and their Laws."

She walked away, robes billowing behind her. Perhaps she'd get more sense from her twelve-year-old apprentice.

Solitude's sprawl didn't just consist of walls and towers. It had dormitories, dining halls and studies enough to house thousands. Over the years, the two hundred Sparkers remaining had concentrated at its hub like warmth at the core of a hypothermic body.

Zanna found Arlo in the Main Library. She smiled as she spied him curled up in a plush, high-backed armchair in front of a roaring fire. She could always rely on him to be found unearthing secrets in the library. Arlo had taken the appearance of the Banished in his stride. He'd made it his quest to discover everything he could about the 'invaders'. It pleased Zanna that her apprentice thought knowledge, not violence, would be their key to survival.

"Find anything?" she asked, collapsing into a chair opposite. He waved a handful of worn parchment at her, covered in black spider scrawl. The old historians never liked to make things easy for them.

"Bits," Arlo replied, a serious look in his bright eyes. "It's funny. I always thought the men of Spring Haven built Solitude when the Banished were pushed north, but I found accounts suggesting it's even more ancient than that. Then, there's this; a journal written by this scholar, Matrim the Mad."

"Well, *he* sounds like a reliable source," Zanna replied, in a solemn voice.

Arlo gave her a withering look. "I'm twelve," he said, "not five. Something's been bothering me about the Banished. There's so many. Where were they?"

Zanna blinked. "A fair question." She tapped her lip. "Their land is small, covered in sparse woods, shale and slate—barren for the most part."

"Well, old Matrim had an answer." Arlo said, leafing through the parchment with excitement. "They discounted his findings because..."

"The whole 'being mad' thing." Zanna helped, tapping tobacco into her pipe.

"Yeah." Arlo nodded. "He writes about spending time with them, about four hundred years ago. Master, he says they lived in the mountain range. Not on it—*inside* it."

Not for the first time, Zanna cursed the lack of real windows in Solitude. No wonder Garet could be so narrow-minded and warlike with only arrow slits to peer through. She pictured the monstrous range that dominated the horizon—the Peaks of Eternity—the largest on the continent. Uncharted.

Except by the Banished, Zanna thought, with a wry smile, *and Matrim the Mad.*

"Any reputable source who'd scouted Banished lands reported primitive, nomadic people," she muttered, lighting her pipe with a flame from her fingertip. "Misdirection? Have they been gathering their forces, waiting for this moment?"

The library's fire crackled and popped. Arlo supplied the only other noise as he shuffled through the ancient parchment.

"Master, do the Banished have the Spark?" he asked, gazing down at a page.

"Before Matrim the Mad's revelations, I'd have said no. But who knows? There's little mention of them in our histories, except to say they were bloodthirsty, violent oppressors, overthrown and chased to the edges of the known world by the combined might of the valiant Haltveldtian armies, before they fractured and Spring Haven 'united' them all once more. A little fanciful, if you ask me. The victors write history."

"Are there other kinds of magic?" her apprentice asked, still staring at the parchment in his hands.

"Not anymore." Zanna crossed her legs and gave Arlo an appraising look. "Legend says the elves used to practice magic that tuned into nature itself. They asked the earth to act and, because of their peaceful nature, it agreed. Before Haltveldt banned it, they mixed and bred with us, so perhaps they lost it then, if they ever had it. Ancient history. Or a myth, I'd wager. As far as I know, and have seen, elves use the Spark like us, though Haltveldt is culling it from them. Slaves with the gift are killed on the spot and their mages are targeted first in battle."

"Nature?" Arlo muttered, biting his lip as he rapped a knuckle against the parchment. "Nature, nature, nature..."

"Did you hear anything I just said?" When he didn't answer, she leaned forward. "What is it?"

Arlo handed the sheet to her. She struggled to decipher the handwriting, but she made out the words 'Banished' and 'magic source.' A coloured drawing covered the page—an enormous stone, covered in moss, with a tree growing out of its middle. Green mist appeared to ooze from a crack running down the centre of the rock. Below it were three words Zanna *could* understand.

THEY WILL RETURN.

"Do you think he meant the Banished?" Arlo asked, eyes wide.

"Drok it all," Zanna spat. "Sparker arrogance strikes again. Matrim the Mad left us a warning in our *own* library."

"Well," Arlo smiled, though fear still lurked behind his bright eyes, "like you said, the whole 'being mad' thing didn't help."

Zanna calmed herself and pushed at her Link to Calene. She'd broken through once but the poor etiquette could be understood under the circumstances. Now, she had to be respectful and knock before entering.

Mother, Calene projected, thoughts clear, strong and sharp. *The Banished appearing doesn't mean we're going to start playing happy families again. What do you want?*

Heat rose in Zanna's cheeks. Her daughter's tone and lingering anger reminded her that her presence remained unwanted.

I don't want to intrude but we must *talk. The Banished wait still. Any change with yours?*

No, Calene replied. *He looked half-starved and near death when we found him, and healing him hasn't woken him up. Not that I expect it to just yet. Is that all you wanted?*

Calene, I have reason to believe they've been planning this for centuries. Zanna looked at the picture with its warning and projected it to her daughter, their Link ensuring Calene would view the drawing with the same clarity she and Arlo did. *Can you copy this? Show it to him when he wakes and tell me his reaction.*

I'll give it a go, Calene replied, and Zanna felt her scorn fade a touch. *Vettigan Linked with his old apprentice in Spring Haven. He's notified the Council and Emperor Locke of our find, and we're heading there now.*

Calene? Be careful.

I've been looking after myself a long time, Mother. And I'd appreciate it if you only contacted me if you have to. I need space...

Calene—

Zanna sighed as her daughter withdrew from the Link. It left her feeling smaller, emptier. Her mind caressed the connection, still pulsing with Calene's essence, as if she could run the back of her finger down her daughter's cheek.

I wish you'd forgive me, Zanna thought, *but how can you if even* I'm *uncertain I deserve it?*

Trumpets echoed through Solitude's hallways and into the library, signalling a gathering of the Sparkers.

"Calene's going to share your discovery," Zanna said, standing and ruffling Arlo's hair. "Stay here. See what else you can find from our friend Matrim the Not-So-Mad."

<hr />

Zanna entered the dining hall and took a seat at a table occupied by several Sparkers near the front of the room. Garet, standing behind the podium, nodded to her as she sat, a triumphant grin on his face.

Zanna slid in beside Miriam, a Sparker who'd visited Solitude fifty years before and never left. Her husband had fallen in a skirmish against elven forces—one in a long line of deaths in the wars to the south. She had always been kind and helped Zanna through the beginnings of her exile. They had often talked long into the night, about Calene, about the elven war, about Solitude and the Spark. She had helped Zanna realise that the fortress could be a sanctuary, not just a prison.

"How goes it with the Banished? Any change?"

"No, they're still gathering in Solitude's shadow, and more of them are trickling in all the time," Miriam whispered, shaking her head. Miriam's copper hair, streaked with iron, swayed as she did. "I walked over the battlements on my way here. They're still minding their own business. It's like there isn't an enormous fortress looming over them."

Zanna watched more Sparkers file in. Around one hundred lived in the immediate vicinity of the central hold, with the others spread out across the far reaches of Solitude's wings. The murmur of whispers built, and soon a buzz of excitement and worry carried through the hall. As soon as the arrivals petered out, Protector Garet cleared his throat and amplified his voice over the hubbub. He held his arms out, palms pointing upwards, like he intended to preach of the gods to them. That'd be a fine sermon coming from him.

"Fellow Sparkers, I'm sure you're all wondering why I've called you here. The Banished wait still, gathering their might." Zanna grimaced as he paused for dramatic effect. "As we speak, our Empire fights a furious and bloody battle with the elven hordes far to the south. This war has drained Haltveldt's resources, as we few, forgotten Sparkers of Solitude know all too well."

A murmur of agreement washed through the hall, though Zanna thought the hum carried its fair share of anger.

"This is about the elves then?" a wizened Sparker across the room cried. "Is the deadlock lifted?"

"In a way..." Garet turned his smile on the room at large. "I've received word from Balz duRegar—the new High Sparker himself—a missive ratified by Emperor Locke Dazel and the Council. The Laws of Engagement are no more. Abolished, in our time of need! We are free to battle how we see fit... to our maximum potential."

The room held its breath a moment, then exploded into a whirlwind of screaming and shouting. Sparkers shot to their feet, waving their fists at Garet and each other, all crying to be heard. Zanna watched Garet, anger rising inside her. The Protector seemed taken aback by the fury he'd provoked. He'd failed to consider an important element in his moment of triumph. Tastes and beliefs had changed throughout Haltveldt—Sparkers lost their faith and conviction in Raas and Janna daily thanks to the elven war and the Empire's constant rhetoric—but old souls filled Solitude, many of them devout out of a form of penitence. They believed in the words of their gods, even if Garet didn't. She remembered their conversation on the ramparts, not an hour earlier.

What would you do, Garet, if the Laws didn't exist?
I would rain fire upon their heads; rend the earth be-

neath them. And if they reached our walls, I would Eviscerate them, so that any who fled would remember what happened the day they challenged the might of Solitude.

"No..." Zanna growled. She called on the Spark, using a little of her own energy and gave her vocal chords a push. "Silence!"

Her voice roared through the hall, drowning out the angry cries of the other Sparkers. One tipped backwards from their bench, landing with a loud crash on the floor. Nervous laughter spluttered in response before dying out.

"You have something to say, Zanna?" Garet smiled. "Perhaps you should seek a pardon from the Council. They may see your perspective now."

He laughed at his own joke, eyes darting around the room to see if anyone joined him. Few did.

"You're planning to attack the Banished?" Zanna replied, getting to her feet and thrusting a finger northward. Beyond Solitude's walls, the plains, where an entire people gathered. "There are children out there, Garet. Unarmed innocents. We don't even know why they're here."

"Our two hundred have no chance against the thousands of Banished with the Laws shackling us. We can't wait for them to attack. Action is faster than reaction." Garet clenched a fist. "We strike first, force the heathens back to where they belong. And, if they don't retreat, we wipe them out, like our ancestors should have."

Another Sparker, Heran, climbed to his feet. He aimed a finger at his throat—needlessly dramatic, Zanna noted—as he amplified his voice.

"Our talents are a blessing, one we use to protect and elevate our kind. So says Raas and Janna themselves." His voice boomed as he gazed around the room. "I've long watched Haltveldt use us as weapons, and I weep to the gods when I see those of our Order playing the part with such ferociousness. To use the Spark in these ways is an affront to nature and the privilege we enjoy. We can hold the Banished in place until Haltveldt's armies arrive but to use forbidden power will bring the wrath of the divine upon us."

"What if we can't?" someone shouted, not bothering with magic to raise their voice. "There are two hundred of us stretched across this gods-forsaken fortress! It'll take all of us to secure it! When are we going to sleep? Eat? How long can we hold the line?"

"What if the Banished have magic of their own and attacking them spells our doom?" Zanna asked, her Spark-infused voice carrying across the hall. She thought of the parchment Arlo had uncovered.

Garet's low chuckle turned into a throaty laugh. This time, other Sparkers joined in. Zanna felt her cheeks burn.

"The Banished's magic?" Garet said, wiping a tear away with a fingertip. "Nonsense. They're primitives. But their numbers are dangerous. Remember, there's nearly half a million out there. Waiting. Watching. If they could muster magic, they'd have attacked years ago. Make no mistake, Zanna, they *will* attack, and even if it's just spears and rocks, all the pretty elemental magic in the world won't save you from the ugly truth. We can't beat them.

Not without *all* the power the gods supposedly gave us."

"We know so little about them," Zanna insisted. "We can't afford to discount anything."

"Rubbish." Garet waved her off. "You're stalling. There's only one question up for discussion here. Do we *attack*?"

"What about Haltveldt's armies?" Miriam asked. She patted Zanna's arm as she did. "Do they march?"

Garet opened his mouth, then closed it.

"Do they march?" Heran cried.

To Zanna's eyes, the Protector appeared to shrink in his robes as every eye in the room turned to him and waited.

"No."

Silence. Heavy, angry, desperate quiet dominated the room. Zanna looked around at her fellow Sparkers; some frowned into the middle-distance, others pursed their lips as they considered the implications.

"Why?" Zanna whispered, her amplified voice turning it into an audible question.

"War with the elves comes first. Many in Spring Haven believe the Banished pose no credible threat. Word from Adhraas says Spring Haven has told them to sit tight and wait. They're...questioning our motives. Saying we're overstating the danger." Garet bowed his head. Then he glanced up at Zanna, fixing her with his cold stare. "Don't you see? This is why we need *all* our power. No one else is going to fight this battle for us. Solitude is my home and

I'm sworn to protect it and everyone inside. I'm sworn to protect Haltveldt and its people. We're too few to stand against the Banished."

"The Emperor has abandoned us?" Heran muttered, slamming down onto his bench, jaw slack.

Zanna glanced at Solitude's leader, then looked away. She despised Garet, but the look in his eye, the pleading tone of his voice, cut into her.

If Calene were here, wouldn't you act? Wouldn't you do anything to protect Arlo?

"A vote," Miriam called.

"Aye," Heran replied, "but not today. We must consider this situation. As Zanna says, the Banished have children among them. We must weigh the will of the gods. We must judge our own souls. In twenty-four hours, we'll decide."

"Sparkers across the Empire unburden themselves of the Laws even as we argue, fighting with all their might against the ravenous elves who seek to destroy them!" Garet cried, desperation in his features. "Would you not allow us to do the same?"

"We are not them," Zanna said, releasing the magic from her throat. "Many here believe in the old ways, we won't abandon them on the Emperor's whim,"

The Sparkers turned to Garet and waited. Solitude's leader took a ragged breath and smoothed the front of his robes.

"Very well," he muttered. "This time tomorrow. Your gods have mercy on us until then."

As he finished, the hall's doors bounced open. Horns sounded from the ramparts and a guard sprinted into the dining hall.

"Masters!" he cried, out of breath. "A party of Banished are approaching the gates!"

CHAPTER FIVE

A DAY FOR THE UNEXPECTED

'The only good elf, is a dead elf.' - A popular saying from
soldiers in the Empire's army.

"Uettigan, is it my imagination or did you use the
Spark to find the most rickety, splinter-rid-
dled, dung-spattered cart in the whole of Colton duchy?"

Calene's mood could have been better. A smattering
of rain fell on occasion this far south, but the heavens had
hammered down, unceasing, since they'd hit the road.
Vettigan had contacted his former apprentice at Spring
Haven, told him of the mysterious Banished. They'd been
instructed to reach the capital 'with all haste', and in complete secrecy.

So they'd swapped their fine steeds for a cart and
mule, their bright Sparker robes for rough, Haltveldtian
travel cloaks—dark, sturdy, nondescript and fragrant,
especially when damp. Their passenger still hadn't woken,
even with the rain. They'd constructed a makeshift canopy
to keep the rain off his face and he wore a relaxed smile

on his lips, though the cart bounced off every rock and pothole on the road.

Calene watched him as she sat in the back, desperate for him to wake but not looking forward to what came next. She held a scrap of paper with the drawing her mother had projected to her—the strange rock with the tree growing from its centre. She'd get answers from the Banished. Somehow.

Calene eyed his broadsword, strapped behind the seats of the cart. It looked in excellent condition, but the fresh nicks in the metal hinted at recent use. Who had he been fighting? And had they lived to tell anyone there was a Banished south of Solitude?

Calene and Vettigan wore their weapons, concealed by their rough spun cloaks. Anything could happen on the road, but they'd only call on their Spark in extreme circumstances. The University trained Sparkers in the art of melee combat because the Laws demanded extreme caution. She enjoyed swordplay but Vettigan accused her of using her blade like a woodcutter used an axe—matchsticks out of pine trees, he said. She returned the favour and called him 'the old dance master'. His flowery fighting style carried too much flourish and pizazz for her tastes, though she acknowledged that not many could best him.

"I'd think you were falling in love with the man if I didn't know better," Vettigan said, glancing over his shoulder, "the way you're staring at him. He's handsome, I suppose."

"More beautiful. There's an innocence about him."

Calene ignored the bait. She kept her love life private, and for an excellent reason. The last time drunken discussion had turned to the topic of romance, she'd made the mistake of mentioning her year-long drought to him. He'd done as friends did and tried to convince every woman in the tavern of her eligibility, including the innkeeper's wife and the bard, who'd been in the middle of her set. They had all asked her why her grandfather arranged her courting for her. Calene had never been so embarrassed, before or since.

"Looking at him, it's hard to believe these are the monsters of old. Grandparents used to say the Banished would steal you away if you didn't behave."

"They'll say the same of the elves," Vettigan grumbled. "We humans say they're inferior to us. Scum. A blight on Haltveldt, and the rest of the world. All they want is the freedom to live their lives. Our children's children will call them monsters to justify our actions."

Calene climbed over the seats and sat next to Vettigan. She lay her head on his shoulder.

"Perhaps that's all the Banished were. Different. Or maybe they were the evil drokers history says, and they've changed their ways. Two thousand years is a long time."

Her head rose as he shrugged.

The road carried them through the Forest of Mists. Tall trees, ancient and proud, reached into the sky and plunged them into twilight, odd for the afternoon. Fog lingered above the ground, thicker in the morning and night, and gave the forest its name. The rain drowned out any other noise, save their creaking cart, but Calene imagined the woods would be alive with birdsong and animal sounds. Water dripped from her hood and caught her nose, and she felt tempted to draw on the Spark and shield their cart from the elements, though that would give them away as magi to any travellers on the road.

Gods' teeth, a breeze wouldn't go amiss either, she thought. A wet heat settled over them like a sodden blanket, making her cloak heavy and her skin sticky.

The intermittent contact with her mother unsettled her, too. Zanna stayed respectful of her boundaries, but Calene felt her brush her mind every so often. A part of her wanted to tell Zanna to back off and leave her alone. Another part craved the comfort her mother provided, the way it used to be.

"Why's it so droking hot?" she complained. "I could cope with rain or the heat on their own, but together? Drok this, I'm not standing for it."

"Beggar, up ahead," Vettigan whispered, laying a hand on her forearm before she could draw on the Spark. "I've no idea how far we are from anywhere in this forest. Let me do the talking."

A figure in a stained, leaf-coloured cloak sat with their back against a tree, a staff lying across their knees. Head bowed, they appeared oblivious to their surroundings. They'd seen several beggars on the road and exchanged food or water for local news and the like. War left many poor and desperate, and Calene hated to see folk go hungry.

"Stranger!" Vettigan called, drawing the cart to a halt, the mule braying. "How far is the nearest village?"

Calene noticed they moved their head away, as if attempting to keep their face hidden. *Taken one too many beatings from travellers I reckon,* she thought, hopping down into the squelching mud.

"We've spare food and water," Calene said, kneeling in front of the stranger. She saw a flash of bright red hair curling under the hood. "We only seek news of the road ahead."

The traveller raised their head a little.

A woman?

The beggar's eyes flicked to the sleeping Banished. Calene noticed the shape of a sword hilt beneath their cloak. She shuffled backwards as the stranger turned their hard stare on her.

"Colton village is another three hours ride from here. Road's bad in places." The woman waited a moment, then asked, "The food?"

"Vettigan?" Calene called, not taking her eye from the slumped figure in front of her. She heard the cart creak and the splat of mud as her companion jumped down and approached. He passed her a package with a small amount of cheese and bread, along with a filled water skin.

"What is he?" the beggar whispered, voice hoarse. Calene couldn't make out her features, but she knew she spoke of the Banished.

She glanced at Vettigan, who shook his head and pointed to the road.

She asks too many questions. His voice bloomed in Calene's mind. *Leave now or we'll have to take steps.*

"Friend of ours," Calene said. "Too much to drink last night. Nasty fall. You know how it is."

"Aye," the stranger replied. "I know how it is."

Calene held the food out in her hands, not wanting to leave the package in the mud. The beggar remained still as rain hammered down around them.

Then her calloused hands snapped out with surprising speed and took the items from Calene.

"Thank you," she said, tucking the food under her cloak and unfastening the water skin.

Calene climbed back into the cart, and turned to watch the beggar as they pulled away, a weight twisting in her stomach. The stranger stood and watched until the forest swallowed them.

◆

They travelled in silence after their meeting with the beggar. The road turned to mud in places, making their progress slow, and daylight faded into dusk.

"I reckon we're an hour from Colton," Vettigan said. "Do we push on, or find somewhere to make camp off-road?"

Calene glanced around, slapping at bugs landing on her face. Since the meeting with the stranger, the Forest of Mists had grown oppressive; the looming trees seemed diseased, their branches reaching out like fingers ready to tear and scratch, the fog thicker.

"Teeth of the gods, push on, man."

"Thought you'd say that," Vettigan grinned, urging the mule forward.

Calene turned, the sound of a soft singing voice catching her attention. The Banished lay awake, gazing at the fading light flickering through the foliage. She couldn't understand the words, but the melody and tone comforted her. Her muscles relaxed at the lilting tune, and the tension she held in her shoulders lessened as she stared into the coiling mist. Memories of happier times with her mother and father, of warmth, comfort and joy flooded her mind. Calene shook her head, bringing herself back into the present.

"Vettigan," she whispered. "When did he wake?"

"I'm not sure," he replied, eyes distant, "but leave him be. Until he stops singing, anyway."

Calene nodded and fought back the urge to leap into the back of the cart and shove the drawing under the Banished's nose. He continued to sing, voice rising and falling like the ocean beyond Sea's Keep on a cool summer's morning.

"Perhaps it's a lullaby?" Vettigan said, voice hushed. "It sounds...familiar. The melody reminds me of something I wish I remembered. A feeling, maybe."

"It's a long journey to Spring Haven. You'll have time for questions...assuming you can figure out his language."

The Banished fell silent, and Calene pulled the picture from her cloak.

"Wait," Vettigan said. "I hear horses."

He steered the cart to the roadside, making space for the approaching travellers. Within seconds, Calene saw them. Two men in bright cloaks riding impressive, strong-looking steeds—Sparkers.

Behind them, a figure draped all in black that drew Calene's eye. The black rider's mount stamped and snorted, agitated. The air appeared darker around the figure, like the forest light seemed afraid to approach, and the thick mist swirled around its hooded head. Whoever lurked beneath the cowl, Calene felt them glaring back.

"Vettigan, well met!" the leader called. Calene squinted at him and recognised his owlish, greying features from Spring Haven.

Ganton, she recalled. *So the other is Zal, his apprentice. And the third?*

Zal drew up alongside his master—blond, with a short beard and superior look on his bold features. Calene knew him by reputation. Wealthy stock, he'd passed in the same childhood circles as Emperor Locke and often sat in on conclave meetings to the impotent outrage of many.

"Ganton, Zal." Vettigan nodded. And he smiled, but Calene picked up a sudden tenseness. "What brings you to the middle of nowhere? And who's your friend back there?"

"A fellow Sparker. We were on our way to the front, when we received word of your discovery. A Banished, a long way south of Solitude." Ganton glanced back at the rider in black, who sat unmoving. Not even the wind stirred its cloak. "High Sparker Balz has instructed us to take the Banished off your hands, and then you're to take the nearest boat to Solitude. The Banished are stirring, and they require reinforcements."

This isn't right, Calene said, Linking to Vettigan. *The one in black... There's hate pouring from beneath that cloak.*

I feel it, too, Vettigan replied.

Zal dismounted and walked towards the back of the cart, ignoring them as if they didn't exist. Calene jumped down and stood in his way.

"You're taking him to Spring Haven?" she asked. He towered over her, sneering down his long nose. Calene glanced behind him, at the rider. "Vettigan asked who your friend is. Aren't you going to introduce us?"

"Didn't you hear High Sparker Balz's orders?" Zal demanded. "We're taking the Banished. We don't have time for uppity foot soldiers."

Calene, her mother spoke into her mind, the sudden Link knocking all other thoughts from Calene's mind, *it's urgent. The Sparkers—*

Bad timing, Mother.

She blocked the connection, and felt her mother's frustration spike before cutting off as she fortified the walls of her mind, keeping it her own.

"Yes, I heard," Calene said, taking a step toward Zal and baring her teeth. "I heard what *you* said his orders were. But how do I know you're telling the truth? It's not like you're being forthcoming, is it?"

The rider in black slid from its horse, hood falling

with the movement. Calene gasped at the sight. A pale, bald woman glared back at her with black eyes. Angry, red cracks ran across her skin. The woman's thin lips curled back into a snarl and Calene felt her draw on her Spark. Zal took advantage of the distraction   and grabbed Calene by the hair. She yelled in outrage as he pulled her face into a rising knee. Her nose exploded on impact and she fell, head ringing. Her vision dimmed as she sank into the cold, wet mud.

"The drok is this?" Vettigan roared.

She looked up at the shout, confused, blood dripping down her face, into her mouth. Her friend leapt from the cart, but froze, sinking to his knees. The Sparker in black moved like a viper, void eyes fixed on Vettigan, a look of deranged glee—no, *desire*—etched into her ruined face. Vettigan shook, eyes wide with fear, shock and disbelief plain in his features.

"Haven't you heard?" Ganton said, licking his lips. He hadn't even dismounted. "Change is in the air. Allow our Shadow Sparker to show you the future."

Calene shook away the pain. Opening the second sight, she gasped. A scream swelled in her throat. Black tendrils oozed from the Shadow Sparker, pulsating as they slithered into Vettigan. They entered his mouth, ears and eyes, and he howled in agony. The Sparker grinned, pulsating as she drained his light. His essence, his energy, seeped into her pores. Calene had seen Evisceration on the battlefield, had seen its after-effects on her father, but nothing like this. The dark energy invading her friend's body seemed a living thing, twisted by the will of this *thing*, this 'Shadow Sparker'.

Vettigan's skin withered, hair shedding from his scalp. Seconds had passed, just seconds, but already he looked a decade older.

"Evisceration?" Calene screamed, wiping the blood from her nose as she struggled to her knees. "You can't do this. Teeth of the gods, are you insane?"

She wouldn't watch this happen again. Not to Vettigan. Not to anyone.

Calene reached deep inside her, knowing she needed to act, that every second counted. She pushed past the pain, used it, sucked her hate, her rage, her *fear* into a pulsing fist inside her. Fed on Vettigan's life, the abomination's Spark grew. If she tried to attack, it would overpower her. Deep down, she knew, her instincts screamed at her. Calene's Spark would only nourish the Shadow Sparker. So she didn't attack it. She improvised. Zanna had always said she had a razor-sharp mind.

She clasped the air, channelling it into a whip, and struck the Shadow Sparker's fussing stallion on the hindquarters. It broke with an outraged whinny and shot past Zal, who had the wherewithal to stagger aside. The Shadow Sparker, lost in the rapture of Evisceration, didn't. The horse trampled the woman into the muddy ground with the sickening crunch of breaking bones.

Vettigan slumped onto his face, body still.

Ganton struck her with the back of his hand, sending her spinning. She hadn't even seen him coming. "You've cost the Empire one of its most powerful weapons, girl. That woman was worth a hundred of you."

Disorientated, Calene crawled in the mud. She watched as Zal climbed into the cart. The Banished stared at her, yellow eyes narrowed and focused, innocence gone. She glanced at Vettigan. He'd flopped onto his front, skin grey, eyes hollow pits staring into the sky. She saw the shallow rise of his chest, but knew he needed immediate healing. Even failed Evisceration could kill. Victims never lasted long, and this had been an Evisceration like no other.

I have to act. Now. The Banished? Or Vettigan?

Calene snarled, forcing herself up. Ganton's boot knocked the air from her as it connected with her stomach, throwing her into the mud once more. He grabbed her by the hair, seized her around her throat, and pulled her to her knees. Calene felt his breath by her ear.

"Watch! After Zal's done with your Banished friend, we'll finish off Vettigan. Then it's your turn."

Zal raised a hand, a black tendril, neither as ravenous nor as insidious as the one the Shadow Sparker commanded, shot out towards the Banished.

It disintegrated.

Ganton echoed Calene's gasp as the Evisceration didn't even make contact, melting away into the air. Zal staggered, the unexpected failure of his magic causing him to flounder. The Banished flowed like water to his feet, a warrior acting with purpose after waiting for his perfect moment to strike. He slammed into Zal and drove him out of the cart and onto the ground. He pulled a dagger from his furs and slammed it into Zal's throat, crimson spurting across their faces.

Calene, Ganton's fist still wrapped around her throat, watched, dumbfounded by the exchange. Evisceration could be cut off if you disturbed the wielder, like all magic, but it never just failed. Not like that. To her, it had looked as though the magic refused to enter the Banished's body, like something inside protected him.

"There are other ways to kill than Evisceration!" Ganton hissed, releasing her.

The ground beneath her feet cracked and she fell to all-fours. Ganton dragged stones from the mud and smashed her to the ground again. Her Second Sight blinked out as the rock cracked her skull. Pain bloomed when she attempted to call her magic. Bile rose in her throat.

The trembling stopped. She blinked through the tears and haze of pain. Zal lay dead and the Banished lay beside him, unconscious. Ganton's volley had knocked him cold. She looked up at the remaining Sparker as he stood over her.

"No one can know of the Banished," he whispered. "I act for Haltveldt and Emperor Locke."

Ganton lifted his hand. A bone-deep weariness washed over her. She wanted to scream as a presence touched her skin, as it tried to force its way into her body. She tried to suck in breath, but the air in her lungs became flame and her vision turned black. Calene's heart beat once—a slow, laboured creak as her fingers and toes curled. The lids of her eyes peeled back. A single word swam to the surface of her retreating mind.

Mother.

Calene gazed at Ganton, whose cold, blue eyes turned black, just the same as the Shadow Sparker's. And she saw the leaves moving behind him.

A red-haired woman unfolded from the trees, sword drawn. An elf.

The beggar from the road!

The elf thrust her sword through Ganton's back. It burst from his chest and blood spattered Calene's face. The Evisceration dissipated. She gasped and fell forward, holding herself up on hands and knees. Ganton had only touched her for a heartbeat, and not with the ferociousness of the Shadow Sparker's assault on Vettigan, but she felt as if she'd run fifty miles without stopping. Her bones ached, her sides stitched, her limbs trembling with the relief of being alive.

Ganton dropped to his knees in front of her. They stared into each other's eyes. He looked confused, crimson bubbling on his lips. The elf swung again and relieved Ganton of his head.

"Thank you," Calene whispered, looking up at the elf.

She didn't hear. She stared past Calene at something behind her, horrified.

Calene spun, skidding in the mud. Vettigan still lay where he'd fallen but the Shadow Sparker had risen from the road, limbs buckled, neck crooked, flesh and cloak perforated by splintered bone and stained with blood. Red dripped from its mouth in a thick stream. It jerked like a marionette as it inched towards Vettigan, black tongue lolling across its lips.

Calene reached out with her Spark, shunning the excruciating pain that wracked her entire body, and pulled on any source of energy she could find. Life bolstered her, chasing away the exhaustion entrenched in her soul, fortifying her will, restoring her. She breathed deep and let it loose, a blast of air with the force of a hammer. It slammed into the Shadow Sparker's body, shattering ribs, rocking it back on its heels. It didn't fall. Instead, it took another staggering step forward.

Calene hit it again. It twisted as the force glanced its shoulder. She heard the joint pop. Still it came. She sucked a breath through her teeth and threw out everything she had with a scream of fury. The Shadow Sparker staggered, then slumped to one knee. Blood streamed from its face. Her attack had scrambled its insides. But it wouldn't die.

It lifted its head, stared at her. She recognised the glint of the Second Sight in its eyes. It could see her Spark. It *wanted* it. Its hand rose towards her.

The elf swept past like a breeze along the forest trail, stirring the leaves in her wake. Calene heard the hiss of her blade cleaving air. The Shadow Sparker's outstretched hand dropped. It toppled.

Calene slumped into the mud, and saw the Shadow Sparker's severed head rolling across the road as the darkness swallowed her.

CHAPTER SIX
A MAN OF HONOUR

*'The Elven Quarter? 'Tis a terrible sight. One day, Avastia will
make the Emperor pay for his treatment of the elves, you mark my
words.'* - An excerpt from a letter intercepted by Emperor Locke's
Inquisition, written by a disgraced Haltveldtian nobleman.

Things had changed in the days since the Emperor's
proclamation and the abolishment of the Laws
of Engagement. The most vocal politicians against the
Sparkers' freedom to act in matters of war had grown
quiet. More than one had experienced a change of mind,
while others had left Spring Haven for their estates in the
country, Master of Coin Uriel among them.

Kade made his way through the bustling streets of
the capital, late for a meeting with Bertrand. The pair had
scrambled to find support for those in Solitude; even with
the relaxing of the Laws, the sheer number of Banished
would overwhelm the defenders, and beyond Solitude
lay Adhraas. The Emperor had authorised no evacuation.
The official word insisted that tales of imminent invasion

from the Banished lands amounted to nothing more than scaremongering.

Kade knew of some within the Sparker Order who had outright refused to join the push against the elves since Emperor Locke's ruling. Bertrand had contacted them, urging them to journey north to lend aid to Solitude. He hoped time favoured them; Kade hadn't received word from Garet or Zanna since the initial flurry of communication, and his thoughts strayed to Arlo. He worried for every soul at Solitude, but his son's fate lay in his and Bertrand's hands.

So long as the Banished hadn't already attacked and swept the Sparkers away.

Kade smashed a fist into his palm in frustration. Octarian spice brought clarity and certainty at first, then anxiety, anger, fear. He'd lost count of the times he'd snapped and snarled in response to innocuous questions. The exhaustion that followed caused him to sleep late into the morning after lying awake most of the night, and had him jumping at shadows even at the best of times. He bit at his fingernails and tasted the sweet tang of the spice beneath. Enough to make his urge for a real fix grow.

The events since the Conclave meeting, and Nexes' apparent knowledge of Kade's past, had him on edge. Glancing at a storefront window as he rushed through Market Street, the major business hub of Spring Haven, the spot between Kade's shoulder blades itched. He paused and watched the reflections for a moment, certain someone followed him.

It's the spice, he told himself, hand straying to the hilt of his sword. *It's rotting your brain.*

Kade had endured a restless night by even his standards; he'd guzzled Avastian brandy and huffed spice as he packed his travel bags. He'd bought passage on a ship leaving Spring Haven after his meeting with Bertrand; room enough for a company of Sparkers.

Too much room, in Kade's mind. He'd approached numerous mercenary groups in the city, seeking to buy an army for Solitude. All had refused his advances as the guild masters prepared to take their bands south to join the push against the elves. He couldn't trump the coin of an Emperor.

"We'll be in more danger from thin ice and bears than your Banished," the first man had told him. The others seemed to share that conviction and Kade had ground his teeth through every round of negotiation until his jaw ached.

If only I had proof, he thought, with a sour twist to his mouth, *though I doubt it would make any difference. The Emperor and his friends seem fixated on the elves, no matter the cost. It's almost as though they* want *Solitude ruined.*

He shook his head. Sometimes, the spice made him feel like conspiracies lurked behind every action.

Bertrand had picked an inn near the harbour for their rendezvous, a place named *Auntie's Blessing.* Kade wasn't familiar with it, but expected a certain atmosphere. The docklands were a law unto themselves within Spring Haven; a hive of scum and villainy. Drink, meat, spice, flesh—

all had its price. Down here, by the water, it came cheap.

The Emperor turned a blind eye to the murders and the power struggles between the various gangs. Kade reckoned the throne collected its taxes in other ways in those muddy alleyways, brothels and taverns. The constant state of flux ensured no gang came out on top. There could be no expansion, no spread of the infection. He appreciated the Emperor's savvy, as much as it disgusted him.

Kade hated this part of the city. Not just the tense, powder-keg atmosphere and rampant crime, but the Elven Gates and the slums beyond them. They'd sprung up centuries before, as a place to keep slaves under watchful eyes and iron heels. The Empire used the elves for labour—construction, repairs, mining and the like—but the people of Spring Haven didn't want them as neighbours. They needed homes, if they could even be called that, but the Empire's obligation ended there.

What better place for filth than a cesspit?

He paused as he reached the giant iron doors leading to the segregated elves. Guards in gleaming armour stood with their backs to the towering walls, and two bright-robed Sparkers sat on stools beside them. A group of loitering citizens hurled abuse—a favourite pastime for many—at any elves passing by, who peered back with black-ringed eyes at the hateful mob before moving on, heads bowed, silent.

As Kade watched, a man, face twisted with vitriol, threw a rock at an elven child who strayed too close to the gate. The projectile struck the child and knocked them down. Blood splashed into the dirt.

"Guards," Kade shouted, pushing his way toward a bored-looking soldier. "Clear this crowd. Now!"

"Drok off, pretty boy," he replied, sneering at Kade, "or I'll rearrange your face until even the wenches around here won't touch you."

He'd dressed in plain clothes—to pass unmolested through the docklands—and looked like anyone else living in lower Spring Haven. He drew himself up and moved his cloak away from the hilt of his sword. Its white-gold pommel caught the sunlight.

"I am Kade Besem, a Master of the Conclave," he said, his even tone filled with icy fury. "Do your duty before I have you whipped. Or better yet, kill you myself."

The guard blinked, eyes dropping to the pommel before glancing at the Sparker sitting by his side. The magi studied Kade's face, then nodded at the soldier. Kade felt a vague sense of recognition, but couldn't place her. He used to have a memory for faces. Before the spice.

"Sorry, sir," the guard said, lowering his eyes. "It's the clothes. You look like a mercenary, is all. Begging pardon, sir."

Kade didn't answer as the man signalled his colleague to join him. He balled his hands into fists and pushed the impulse to fight down into his gut.

I wanted that fool to give me an excuse, he thought, drawing a deep breath. His anger still bubbled beneath the surface.

"This is fine with you?" Kade growled, turning his

frustration on the female Sparker instead. "Children assaulted while you sit and watch?"

The Sparker's eyes turned cold. "They're fortunate we give them somewhere to live," she responded, summoning fire into her hand and staring into the flames, "and we don't go in there and wipe them out like the vermin they are."

Kade spat at her feet, and she smirked back. He approached the gate and kneeled, eyeing the stricken elf—a boy, not much older than Arlo.

The child picked himself up off the ground and stared at Kade, a thin, gnarled hand pressed against the wound on his forehead. Blood seeped through his bony fingers. He wore rags caked in filth, blond hair smeared brown with dirt, high cheekbones so sharp they almost poked through his stretched, pallid skin.

"Here," Kade said, pulling a clean handkerchief from his cloak. His hand shook as he held it through the gates. "I'm sorry. It's all I can offer."

The boy watched him, before taking a slow step forward on trembling legs. He snatched the cloth from Kade's hand and pressed it against his head.

"I hate you," he mumbled, voice cracked and hoarse. "All of you."

"I know," Kade whispered, tears welling as he thought of Arlo trapped behind those bars, in that place. "I don't blame you."

Their eyes met for a second, and Kade saw the shadow of his son. Instead of love, mistrust and animosity stared back.

The child turned and staggered away. Kade scanned the slums beyond the walls. He knew the elves lived deeper in the shantytown, but the place seemed deserted now. Elves loved the forests, the rivers, the hidden, beautiful places of the world. Even the finest palace in Spring Haven would have been a prison to them.

Kade sighed. For an elf, only servitude to a wealthy household could save them from the slums, but it still meant slavery. Like Arlo's mother, Rune.

She'd been a servant in his family's service and he'd found himself smitten the day he'd returned home from the guildhall to find her working there. It might have been her maturity—he'd still been a boy, more or less, and her ageless in the elven way—or perhaps the way she didn't seem to find him charming in the least. Different from all the other girls he'd known. Her disdain hadn't curdled his interest. Instead, it had only made him determined to prove how different he could be. The turning point had come when he'd stopped the steward whipping another slave for stealing bread. Kade had insisted he'd been the thief. Then he'd pilfered even more bread and brought it to her.

He stole any time alone with her he could. Rune would tell him of her childhood home, in the Forest of Mists, before the Haltveldtian Empire had driven the elves further south. Before they'd captured her.

He'd pledged to run away with her, once they were married, and he'd meant it. He'd been ready to leave it all behind—Spring Haven, his home, his career, all of it—but when Rune had fallen pregnant, he'd told her they could trust his parents. That they'd see the truth in their love and provide for their grandchild. Rune hadn't believed him but she'd stayed anyway.

She'd been right. His parents hadn't seen the truth. And, when Rune had died, they'd called it a blessing of the gods.

In the years since, Kade's reputation had suffered as his family circulated stories of a baby left on his doorstep after a night of youthful passion at a brothel. The strength of the Besem name ensured him a place in the Conclave— as the first son, he had a duty to represent his family's interests—but the role of Liaison to Solitude served as a mark of his indiscretion. His parents hadn't complained. Kade suspected they'd been the hand to slap his wrist.

His embarrassment didn't matter. The need to keep Arlo safe outshone his ego. Except that now Arlo stood between Haltveldt and the Banished hordes, and Master of War Nexes knew their secret.

"Be careful what side you're on," the Sparker said, as Kade walked past. The fire danced in her hands. "Elves and their friends will get theirs soon."

<hr />

Kade ducked into an alley and leaned against the wall. The *Auntie's Blessing* lay close, but the sun beat down on him and his hands shook. He told himself the experience at the elven gates had unnerved him, and it had, but Kade knew the truth.

I'm an addict, he thought, glancing around to see if anyone watched.

He couldn't shake the nagging sensation of eyes on him the whole journey to the docklands, but whoever might have been following him didn't enter the alley.

He took his snuffbox from his cloak and held it to his nose, the container shaking below his nostrils. He breathed the drug's powerful aroma, let it flood his senses. Within seconds, his strength returned—colours swelled and deepened, and the hubbub from the city sang in his ears like music. He let out a ragged sigh, straightened and wiped the sweat from his brow with his cloak.

"I'll give it up," he muttered, concealing the box, "as soon as I save Solitude."

Kade strode into the *Auntie's Blessing* and took in the scene. Drunken sailors drank more, played cards and called for music though the sun had only risen a few hours before. It didn't matter the time of day at places like this— alcohol, food, music and sex flowed to anyone with the coin to pay. A fight broke out in the corner and one sailor picked up a chair and slammed it across the back of another. A brawl ensued and Kade moved, unnoticed, towards the warren-like backrooms.

People of all stations and walks of life conducted business in places like this. The brothels drew many from the Conclave and higher society. Wasn't Kade supposed to know that better than most? Bertrand's message told Kade to look for room one hundred and eight. The inn had three floors, and the place he needed lay up two flights of stairs.

Kade passed an open window and looked out at the harbour. Sunlight sparkled off the sea's surface and he could taste salt on the air as seagulls wheeled and shrieked.

Such a beautiful day, Kade thought, walking toward his destination, *or is this what they call the calm before the storm?*

Knocking once on door one hundred and eight, Kade pushed inside.

"Bertrand, I hope the news is good. I've a ship ready to—"

The words died on his lips.

Destruction lay about him; broken chairs and tables strewn across the floor, scorch marks on the walls and blood leading towards the bedroom. Kade drew his sword and followed the trail. He closed his eyes and braced himself as he nudged the door open.

Bertrand's body lay on a crimson-soaked bed, wide eyes staring at the ceiling and face twisted in a rictus of agony.

Kade heaved and vomited on the floor as he took in Bertrand's remains. They'd stripped him naked and tied his wrists and ankles to the four corners of the bed. Angry cuts and gashes covered his limbs, face and chest. His torturer had ripped his stomach open and his intestines hung from the gaping wound. A dagger jutted from his left eye—the finishing blow—and Kade held no doubt Bertrand would have welcomed it.

He wiped his mouth on his sleeve. His eyes wouldn't stop watering. The stench of death hung heavy in the room—rusted iron and voided bowels. Kade ran to the window and flung it open.

"Raising rebel Sparkers to your cause. That's treason, Master Besem."

Kade spun. Master of War Nexes threw the bedroom door shut and leaned against it. Blood splattered his tanned face and coated his gloves up to his forearms. Unlike Kade's rough spun travel clothes, he'd dressed in black silk to do his butcher's work. A frenzied fire lit his eyes. He looked at Bertrand and smiled, like an artist admiring a masterpiece he'd just finished. It made the bile rise in Kade's throat again.

"Bastard," Kade growled, levelling his sword.

"Kade," Nexes said, flicking his cloak aside. He wore a short sword on each hip. "Bertrand confessed. Treason of the highest order. It took a little while but we got there in the end. He bucked against the Imperial decree to focus all our strength on the elves. He died a traitor's death, as all who defy our Emperor must. *All*."

"You've gone too far, Nexes!" Kade cried, jabbing a finger at Bertrand's corpse. "Why do *this*? You're already pushing the elves back. They wouldn't have lasted long, even before the Emperor abolished the Laws. You'll get what you want, so why kill Bertrand? Why stop us from reinforcing Solitude? You're condemning them all to death!"

"Yes," Nexes agreed, drawing his weapons. He dropped into a duellist's stance, holding the short swords at different levels in front of his body. "The Banished are on the move. One's appeared in the south, if you can imagine. Well beyond Solitude's gates."

Kade blinked, jaw dropping loose before he snapped it shut. "Banished in the south? If the threat is real, why let them attack? Solitude can't stand against a massed army with so little to defend it!"

He surveyed the room, looking for an advantage. He found nothing. Nexes' reputation for swordsmanship suggested he may as well piss in the wind.

"These words won't mean much to you, but it's for the greater good. We know more about the Banished than you realise. Much more. Try to take some solace in that before you meet the gods."

"I'll spit in their teeth before I find comfort in anything you say," Kade snarled.

Wind ruffled his cloak. He remembered the open window at his back and the harbour below. *It's a three-storey drop. But it's offering better odds than this fight.*

Nexes took a step into the centre of the room, giving himself room to swing and parry.

"War drives the nation. It allows our citizens to forgive our more... aggressive inclinations." He smirked at Kade and his tongue lashed the blood from his lips. "The elves are our enemy for now, our focus, but their time is almost at an end. Next, we turn to the Banished. After news circulates of the horrors they've inflicted on Solitude, Haltveldt will cry for bloody vengeance. Then, with the continent united, north and south, we'll look beyond our shores. Make the foreign nations quail at our name. Our strength!

It's a shame about your son up there in Solitude...though he is part-elf. Trust me, it's all for Haltveldt. To ensure our survival."

Kade snarled and drew his sword arm back, flinging the weapon at Nexes. He suppressed a flicker of satisfaction as the Master of War dived aside to avoid it. The sword slammed blade-first into the door, jamming it shut, and Kade jumped out of the window.

He fell two storeys and landed on a taut canopy below. He bounced off and hit the cobbles. His leg twisted with a sickening crunch. Pain exploded as his ankle crumpled beneath his weight. People turned to stare as he screamed through gritted teeth.

He didn't want to look, but he couldn't help himself. His foot pointed in a different direction to his shin. Blood pooled under it. Fighting against the pain, he fumbled for his Octarian spice and shoved the box under his nose. The drug would help with the pain.

Through the tears, Kade glanced up at the window he'd leapt from. Nexes stared down at him. The sword jammed through the door would keep him trapped long enough for Kade to run, unless he jumped too. He suspected Nexes had more sense than that but, as Master of War, he had soldiers who could pick Kade up from the street.

He had to move.

"The docks," he muttered, his head swimming as the spice did its work and the pain in his ankle lessened. "I can make it."

Struggling to his feet, he limped into the crowd, stumbling and hopping. He staggered into a dockworker, who shoved him back. The spice box slipped from his hand and vanished into the press of milling bodies.

"No!" Kade cried, dropping to his knees, snarling against the throb of anguish at the sudden change of direction.

He saw the box on the floor, close enough to reach. He stretched for it, fingers aching just to hold it, then a foot connected with it and sent it spinning out of sight.

Kade bit his lip, hands curling into fists, sweat beading on his forehead. He *needed* that spice. For the pain. For courage.

How could he do any of this without it? How could he save Arlo? How could he remember Rune without weeping?

Find the box! Without the box, you're nothing!

No. He had to move. He had to reach the docks, board the boat to Solitude. The Empire would let the fortress fail, and kill every soul within its walls, his son included.

With a snarl, Kade struggled to his feet, and limped towards the docks with as much speed as he could muster.

He had hoped to bring a company of fighters to save Solitude. A lone drug addict would have to do. His son needed him.

CHAPTER SEVEN
THE CRADLE

'Never forget what we fought for, and who battled by our side. Ignore the Cradle's knowledge at your peril.' - A warning from the Sparker Trell, one of the Cradle's founders, taken from the Book of Memories. Her message went unheeded.

"Wait here," Nexes Almor commanded his retinue.

Haltveldt's Master of War dismounted his horse and removed his riding gloves, glancing at the eucalyptus trees surrounding him. The sun's heat added a sheen of sweat to his skin, but he paid it no mind. The faint sounds of the sea helped to push the morning's vexations from his mind.

Kade Besem escaping hadn't been part of the plan.

Still, Nexes thought, adjusting the sword strapped to his waist, *what can one man do? He's a drug-addled, elf-loving traitor. It would surprise me if the fool realises where he is when he surfaces from his spice haze.*

The fact that he'd escaped didn't rankle so much—people got lucky—but that sword throw had caught

Nexes by surprise. He'd underestimated the man and the Master of War prided himself on knowing every detail, every weakness, of anyone holding a position of power in Haltveldt. He'd thought Kade would crumple at the sight of Bertrand's butchered body. That he'd roll onto his back and show his belly like a cur.

Won't make the same mistake twice. A smile broke out across Nexes' face. After his men lost Kade in the crowd, he'd acted with speed, and taken steps. *The Emperor's strategy in the north remains unaltered.*

Nexes strode with cat-like grace through the 'Emperor's Gardens'—a place forbidden to all save the Emperor and his closest advisors. He nodded to black-robed Sparkers who waited in the shade. Trained in secret and loyal to the Emperor, they ensured the garden remained private. The Conclave might have repealed the Laws of Engagement mere days ago but they had been years in the making. These brave souls had been among the first volunteers. True patriots. They shared the Emperor's priorities, his vision for a stronger nation.

Shadow Sparkers, they called them. Nexes appreciated the theatrical name; the mere mention of them would soon strike fear into the heart of anyone who opposed Haltveldt.

Their robes matched their souls; Nexes had watched their appearances twist as they perfected their dark arts on enslaved elves, political prisoners and other Sparkers who didn't appreciate the march of progress—they lost their hair, eyes turning black as pitch, their skin blistered and cracked. They were the Emperor's little secret, and the shape of things to come.

Nexes met the eyes of one but looked away as he caught his reflection in those black pits. He always thought they saw too much. More even than the other Sparkers with their Second Sight.

They're useful, Nexes thought, hand falling onto the hilt of his sword. The feel of cold steel comforted him. *But there's something inhuman lurking behind those stares. Perhaps the dissenters are correct; twisting the Spark changes you. A necessary evil.*

The shade from the trees granted welcome relief from the sun, beating down on Spring Haven without mercy, but Nexes knew he'd have to leave its comfort soon. His destination approached, and the crash of waves grew louder. Through the foliage, he saw a figure standing at the cliff edge. High Sparker Balz duRegar, his face tilted towards the sun as if basking in its presence.

Nexes drew alongside him and glanced to his side. A stone stairwell led down the cliff's face and into the cave that housed the Cradle. Few even knew this place existed, its location passed down from Spring Haven's first ruler, all the way to Emperor Locke himself. Balz, being close to the Emperor, had been brought to the ancient library long before he ascended to his current position of High Sparker.

"Nexes, well met," Balz murmured. Nexes turned to see his friend smiling at him. Scars had etched into the man's face over the last months. The cost of power. "The Emperor's below, delving through those ancient tomes.

I'm not sure what else he expects to find."

Nexes gripped Balz's shoulder. "We come to the crux of it, my friend. The moment Spring Haven has worked towards since old Emperor Caslo rediscovered this place. It's natural our Emperor would linger here."

Accounts of Caslo had it that he'd executed anyone who learned of the Cradle's existence, judging the information it held too valuable, too incendiary, for anyone else to know. Only an Emperor could hope to wield that knowledge responsibly, he'd said.

"Aye," Balz replied, turning to the waves crashing below.

Nexes could see Spring Haven in the distance—fifteen miles away, all told—towering over the shoreline. Its beauty, a jewel standing out from the drok of Haltveldt, never failed to take his breath away.

"Word reached me about the trouble at the docks earlier. Should I send...assistance?"

"All is well, my friend." Nexes forced a smile. Bad enough Kade got away. Word spreading of it made matters worse. The Master of War didn't appreciate slights against his reputation. "Are you joining us in the Cradle?"

Balz shook his head. "No, I'll stay a while out here. I feel the eyes of the dead watching me when I'm in that place. Their voices echo in my mind."

"You're getting superstitious in your old age," Nexes laughed, clapping him on the back.

"Swine," Balz replied, with a wink. "You're a month older than I. I'll leave it to you and our Emperor to delve the Cradle's secrets."

"They won't stay secret for long."

Nexes smiled and took a step towards the staircase, then paused as he glanced over his shoulder towards his friend.

"You're not worried about Solitude, are you?" he asked, studying Balz's face. A shadow crept across it as he continued to stare out to sea. "We exiled your father there, after all. He faces death without the aid of our armies."

The silence stretched as Balz gazed at nothing.

"I hadn't thought of him," he said, with a shrug. Not entirely truthful. "Solitude's destruction is unavoidable. Today, tomorrow, or fifty years from now, its fate is written. We must allow it to play out then rise to meet the threat, united under Haltveldt's banner."

A gentle breeze nipped at Nexes' cheeks as he descended the stairs carved into the cliff side. He peered at the rocks below, and thoughts of slipping and plummeting to his death forced their way into his mind. He slowed his steps and wondered if anyone had ever suffered such a fate. Maybe during Caslo's days.

Relief bloomed in his chest as he ducked into the cave. The Cradle lay before him. A faded mosaic floor greeted him, whatever it depicted lost to time and the salt in the air. It led to a balcony that overlooked rows of shelves stacked with books, parchments and drawings stretching back to the time of Raas, Janna and the so-called nameless gods. The Cradle revealed those names, and so much more.

Nexes cast his mind back to when he'd first laid eyes on the place, the wonder that filled him, the privilege of

knowing what so many didn't. Those emotions had long
dulled, replaced with the weight of understanding and
responsibility. Still, he wouldn't leave this task to anyone
else.

*They aren't strong enough to shoulder this burden. We
are.*

Crimson drapes hanging from the ceiling displayed
an emblem of a shield with a green stone embossed in
its centre—not Haltveldt's coat of arms but something
entirely different—a curious detail the Cradle didn't ex-
plain. Above the stacks, a golden globe floated, the world's
continents etched into it. Nexes glanced at Haltveldt and
let his eyes follow the contours as unseen energies allowed
the sphere to spin in a slow, endless dance.

He watched as the vast lands of Octaria, Velen and
beyond revealed themselves, still turning to the secret
continent lurking behind the Avastian islands before it
returned to Haltveldt. His country, alone and surrounded
by enemies.

Nexes imagined what armies the Octarian and Velen
nations could call upon to invade Haltveldt and ground his
teeth. His grand nation appeared tiny in comparison. He
knew the Avastians lived alongside elves, and shuddered
at the thought of those races living as one, and the fury
they could inflict on Haltveldt at a moment's notice. He
mulled over the secrets of the unnamed lands beyond, so
enormous they could swallow Haltveldt a hundred times
over.

"So many threats," Nexes muttered, gripping one of

his short swords. His eyes narrowed as the globe continued to spin. Above it, a banner proclaimed the mantra he repeated to himself each morning, as he peered into his mirror, to remind himself of the stakes. "One Haltveldt, One Nation."

He heard a rustle and peered between the stacks below. Emperor Locke leaned against the end of a row as he unrolled a parchment, lost in its secrets. With one last, narrow-eyed glare at the globe and its promises of annihilation, Nexes descended to the lower level, oil lamps guiding his way in the Cradle's gloom.

The Emperor had first brought Nexes to the Cradle some thirteen years before, when they'd made their decision to supplant Emperor Locke's father. The old Emperor had shared the Cradle's secrets with his son not long before. It had been his call to arms. A deadlocked war with the elves, a military in disrepair and Sparkers who lived their lives as preachers and healers rather than warriors. If the Cradle's revelations turned out to be true, what chance would they have?

Young Locke's bitter arguments with his father had strained their relationship. It had become clear that the old Emperor didn't have the strength to do what had to be done. Haltveldt needed a new leader. Nexes had always respected Locke for his ambition, his iron will, his clarity and focus. He'd respected him all the more when he smothered the old man with a pillow in the middle of the night and took the throne with his own hands.

It had been Nexes who'd suggested bringing Balz into

the fold. They'd needed a Sparker, and who better than their old friend? They'd spent the first week after Locke's coronation delving through the histories, and futures housed in the ancient library.

It had revealed so much. The Haltveldtians of Spring Haven who'd forced the Banished north had created the Cradle, a library built by both mundane and magical means, founding the place so that their history didn't vanish into the mists.

Well-intentioned, they might have been, but they hadn't counted on what happened next. The alliance crumbled and descended into warfare. Petty arguments and mistrust were rife in the years after they'd ended the Banished threat. The Cradle lay forgotten, until Spring Haven's first Emperor, Caslo, rediscovered it.

Nexes suspected it had spurred him into expanding Spring Haven from a single city-state into a continental power. He and his descendants brought the other duchies under their rule, one after another. Under Caslo's leadership, the Sparkers founded the University and manned Solitude once more. The seeds of an Empire.

He'd learned much about the Banished too. Called the First People, they ruled Haltveldt and subjected the humans and their elven helpers to cruel domination. They used the Spark as they saw fit, and had even exiled their gods, Raas and Janna, from their lands, though Nexes had found some accounts that claimed the First People had slain them. He shook his head at that, and wondered what the worshippers of Raas and Janna would think if they knew.

Somehow, the First People suffered defeat, a crucial detail missing. Nexes had scoured the records for some inkling of how, but came up short. But the Cradle revealed more still.

Sparkers with the Future Sight, a talent that had died out over the ages, had revealed prophecies, creating moving dioramas housed in alcoves built into the Cradle's walls. They predicted crucial events—war, famine, drought and sickness—some of which had even come to pass within living memory. Only one prophecy remained now, one Nexes felt certain they were witnessing in their own lifetimes. After, they would be left to flounder in the dark. Nexes would have put the founders to the sword for that indignity if he could.

The ancient place still held secrets. A twenty-foot-high, circular stone door stood at the Cradle's deepest point. Curious glyphs of a language forgotten by man were carved upon it. The doorway glowed with a faint green light that never changed. No other illumination appeared to alter it. And it wouldn't open.

Previous emperors had tried and failed to uncover the Cradle's final mystery. They'd detailed their attempts in the Book of Memories, a tome that lay in the Cradle's hub and documented Haltveldt's history as its rulers saw it.

The Emperor and his friends had tried brute strength, invention and Balz's Spark to pry it open with no success. Now, the Emperor ignored it. Nexes couldn't. It always drew his eye when he visited. As a man who considered every angle, the things that lay beyond the door gnawed at him.

Approaching the Emperor, still consumed by his re-search, Nexes' eyes flicked to one of the dioramas on the wall. The final one. It depicted Solitude, an army beyond it, shifting and changing to show the invaders breaking through. As the horde pushed on, a lone figure waited for them. Words appeared, separating the single shape from the onrushing enemy. Nexes didn't need to read them; they were etched in his soul.

"With the Fair Ones on their knees, the First shall return, and ruin with them," Nexes murmured, his voice carrying through the silence, his stare flicking to the stone door that still kept its secrets. "One nation, one Haltveldt. He born apart, shall be its salvation. Protect him."

"Nexes," Emperor Locke said, without looking around. "You know I love it when you talk about me."

"Or your son," Nexes replied, coming to a halt at a respectable distance.

Nexes held no doubt the prophecy referred to one of them. Nothing set someone apart more than royal blood.

After viewing the words for the first time, and seeing that those events were the only ones yet to occur, their triumvirate had become convinced that the time of the Banished's return drew near.

Their predecessors had spent years playing down the Banished threat. After all, the final prophecy would never be their concern. They were happy to live out their lives safe in the knowledge that the events would be after their time. Before Emperor Locke, Haltveldt's rulers had lost faith in the Cradle's warnings; or maybe they'd just been too comfortable, too bloated from luxury and excess, too *lazy*. The people of Haltveldt had believed them because ignorance came easier. Only they three understood and they had studied the Cradle's every offering to find a way to make Haltveldt whole. The first step would be ending the war with the elves—the Fair Ones—for good.

The Cradle's archives claimed humans and elves had once been allies against the First, but Emperor Locke had ruled out a truce. Elves were subhuman scum, untrustworthy, and they would accept peace only until the Empire turned its back. Their hatred for the humans of Haltveldt ran deep. They had to be destroyed, wiped out, before Haltveldt could face the threat from the north. They couldn't afford to leave the Banished potential allies. They'd run back to their old masters in a heartbeat if they thought it would save them from extinction.

Nexes, as Master of War, agreed. He'd supported Emperor Locke's propaganda against the elves, fomenting hatred and distrust so that Haltveldt's citizens would meet the elves genocide with celebration. The army's ranks swelled and the Sparkers embraced the full extent of their powers, all to end the ancient enemy. Together with the Emperor, Nexes redoubled Haltveldt's war efforts and they had broken the seemingly endless deadlock. The days of elves on their continent were numbered.

The sudden return of the Banished—the First People—came as no surprise. Now, they had to make the rest of Haltveldt believe in the danger after centuries of thinking them nothing but simple shepherds and bogeymen of legend, and nothing did that better than a tragedy.

The fall of Solitude and two hundred Sparkers is a small price to pay, Nexes told himself. *A sacrifice for the greater good. And, if Adhraas falls soon after, then it's an even greater tragedy to light vengeful fury in Haltveldt's heart.*

"Yes," Emperor Locke muttered, looking up from the parchment in his hands. "My son. He's a little young to be a saviour, no?"

"Unless this war lasts decades," Nexes replied, with a tight smile.

The Empress had given birth to their heir two months previous. High Sparker Balz had presided over his naming. Locke II, next of the Locke Dynasty, a brave new tradition.

The two men clasped hands. "Let's hope not." The Emperor grinned. "But war has been good for us. The trouble with peace is that it makes people soft. It gives them time to think about their rights, what they're *entitled* to. War keeps everyone pliable. Ready. Strong. It speeds progress and that's what Haltveldt needs. We couldn't have abolished the Laws without the elven war as an excuse, and we'll need that power in the battles to come."

"And once news of the massacre at Solitude reaches the cities, the people will beg for us to do whatever's necessary. As will any dissenting Sparkers. And, if they disagree, I'm sure the Shadow Sparkers will change their minds."

"What of these 'dissenters'? Did you discover their names?"

"Yes, my Emperor," Nexes said. He scowled inwardly at the thought of Kade Besem's escape at the port. "Our very own Master of Ceremonies, Bertrand, and his friend, Kade Besem, rallied around fifty names to their cause. Bertrand is dead, and the rest will follow before too long. Kade escaped on a vessel heading towards Adhraas. It's in hand."

The Emperor nodded, his over-large features growing solemn. He rolled up the parchment he held.

"This scroll interests me, Nexes. Do you recognise it?"

Nexes inclined his head. He'd seen the Emperor reading it often, but he could see his friend wanted to talk about it, and Nexes served his Emperor's will.

"A Sparker named Trell wrote it, about two thousand years ago. She fought the First People. She wrote about their depravity and helped create this place so we wouldn't forget. But we did! We fought against other human cities and lost sight of the real enemy. The First People, and their helpers, the elves. Slaves, yes? But we both know slaves serve a master."

Something in that gave Nexes pause. Emperor Locke was his master. So what did that make him?

"If our ancestors hadn't lost this place, if they'd united Haltveldt sooner, if they'd obliterated the elven scourge as they should have from the beginning, we could have marched beyond Solitude and put an end to the First People before they returned. Hope for peace has sickened and softened our Empire. War is what Haltveldt requires, and we have so many enemies. Fighting amongst ourselves makes us weak. Dissent makes us weak. I worry, Nexes. I do."

"About what, my Emperor?" Nexes asked, though he knew, and shared, those same concerns.

"When Solitude falls, our enemies overseas will strike. Halting trade with them won't stop them hearing word of the invasion. They'll see us as weak, ripe for the taking. We must strike the Banished hard, without mercy and with *haste*. To that end, I require you to travel south. See that the elves are dealt with, once and for all. You're the Master of War, after all. Inspire our brave soldiers. Unleash our Shadow Sparkers, and let the others follow their lead. Make sure they know that not a single elf can remain. Then, take our armies north and do the same to the Banished when they cross the Peaks of Eternity. Show them our might. Let the other nations tremble when they see the fate that awaits our enemies."

"Your word is law, my Emperor," Nexes replied. He saluted and spun on his heel.

"Nexes? My friend?"

"Yes, my Emperor?"

"Don't fail me now. For Haltveldt."

"Always."

Nexes strode through the library, his thoughts already turning to the elves. Soon, only the Cradle would remember them and Haltveldt would be a nation whole. As prophesied. The one born apart would lead them to salvation, and Nexes would do everything in his power to aid him, his Emperor.

Walking past the diorama, Nexes glanced at it and smiled.

"The First People will regret leaving their mountains," he said, gazing at the lone figure standing in their way. "I'll make certain of that."

CHAPTER EIGHT
SOLITUDE'S SHADOW

'Give someone with power a bit more, and you'll create a tyrant.' -
An ancient proverb, one Haltveldt's noble families place
little stock in.

"The Banished sure like waiting." Arlo said, peering over the battlements.

Zanna nodded, a frown etched into her forehead. Their army waited, same as ever, except that now a party of twelve Banished lingered outside the walls, staring up at the ramparts. It seemed they'd marched all the way from the Peaks of Eternity just to wait.

The sentry's warning had stirred the Sparkers into a panic but the storm had blown itself out before it even started. It hadn't been the attack Garet wanted. The stalemate remained.

She peered through her telescope at the dozen who'd approached. A mixture of male and female, the pale Banished watched back. Studying them, she noticed that they deferred to one who stood at the head of the group. He wore an uncomplicated bronze crown atop his white hair, though the mighty broadsword strapped to his back suggested the Banished leader could fight. She doubted she could have wielded a weapon that size without her Spark.

Zanna swept her gaze across the plains; stragglers trickled over the foothills and joined the ranks of the assembled Banished.

"Perhaps they won't act until the rest join them. Are you scared, Arlo? It's okay if you are. Natural."

The boy bit his lip and placed his own telescope to his eye.

"At first. I thought they'd kill us all. But I listen to them sing at night, and it soothes me when I wake from my nightmares."

"It is beautiful," Zanna agreed, ruffling her apprentice's hair and eyeing him with concern.

The boy had spoken of nightmares since arriving at Solitude, but never wanted to talk about them. He even grew angry when Zanna pressed him. She decided to let him talk when he felt ready. She'd learned her lesson with Calene.

Each night, the Banished's songs filled the air, melodies that broke her heart, then mended it even as she wept. They reminded her of Calene. Her daughter enjoyed singing, or had. They'd played instruments together, when she'd been a child, though Zanna always preferred listening to Calene sing from her heart.

I don't know what she likes anymore, Zanna thought. *My daughter's a stranger to me.*

She pushed against the connection they shared again, but hit upon the barrier her daughter had erected. Zanna had contacted her the day before—right after Garet had told them of the Conclave's ruling on the Laws of Engagement—but Calene had cut her off. There could have been myriad reasons but the lingering silence fed her fears. She pushed at the barrier one more time, found it impassable, and sighed.

At least she's alive, Zanna told herself. *There wouldn't be a barrier to touch otherwise. Though I doubt the Banished she healed will survive long in Spring Haven.*

The capital's appetite for war sickened her. Their willingness—no, eagerness—to use the most terrible part of the Spark as a weapon signalled a descent into wickedness. Her husband had wanted it too. Ricken had taken an evil path. He'd seen the Spark as a tool to dominate and rule. He'd experimented on others, pushing their limits and his own.

Zanna hadn't noticed his descent until too late. Their duties as Sparkers had kept them apart for months at a time. The depths he'd sunk to only became clear the day he'd turned his attention to their daughter. Calene's power blazed like a bonfire on a dark night. Or the fire of a burning city.

"Will I see my father again?" Arlo asked.

He stared up at Zanna, tears in his eyes. She forgot his young age at times. It pleased her that she could talk to him about Kade. Only she and Garet knew where Arlo had come from, and the Protector didn't seem to notice the boy's presence most of the time.

"I'm certain," she said, smiling back. "He'll change the Conclave's mind. An army will arrive, and we'll survive until they do."

She put a brave face on it for his sake. In truth, she worried. Kade Besem's past haunted him, just as Zanna's did. Rumours swirled about his son's origin—tales of sordid affairs, incest and murder. As she watched Arlo scan the horizon, Zanna knew the truth. Kade and his son would suffer if people discovered his mother had been of elven descent. Only execution awaited an elf with the Spark. Kade's plan to send him to Solitude with her made sense, though she worried it just delayed the inevitable.

Thunder rumbled in the distance and lightning danced across the cloudless sky. Zanna draped her arm across Arlo's shoulders and drew him close.

"I suppose I should go vote," Zanna murmured, as Arlo pressed his head against her side. "They won't let you, I'm afraid. Too young."

Not that it seemed to matter. Arlo's life hung in the balance, just the same as every other Sparker in Solitude. Why not let him decide his own fate?

The boy remained silent.

"What is it?" she asked.

"Why did you Eviscerate someone, Master? What happened? I mean, you told me someone attacked your daughter, but... You can use the Spark in so many ways. Why that way?"

Zanna didn't answer at first. Campfires began to

bloom among the Banished in the dying of the light. Their singing began, mixing with the thunder. The air cloyed, and she thought she smelled rain in the air.

"Calene hadn't fulfilled her potential yet, even though she'd turned twenty-two. I'm still not sure she's reached her limit, even now. Her Spark is vast. Greater than any I've seen other than... Well, that doesn't matter. My husband, Ricken, wanted to see how far he could push her. He thought like Garet, and too many others, that our power meant we should rule. He grew cruel but I didn't notice until it was already too late. He attacked me—his wife, his *friend*—left me for dead.

"I awoke as he experimented on Calene. I don't know what happened, I just...lashed out. Part of me wanted to stop, but I couldn't. Not until I'd devoured everything that made him. I felt him fade. His soul, his essence... I fed on it. Drew it inside me. Fear drove me on. Fear that he'd never stop unless *I* stopped him. And something else. Hatred. Every ill-feeling, every tiny resentment, I'd ever felt towards him, towards myself, magnified in that moment.

"I watched him melt before my eyes, but I'd given in, and the darkness that lives in all of us... It wouldn't let me stop until it had eaten its fill."

She remembered that night, so clear. Calene, helpless. Ricken, ravenous. She'd have burned the world to a cinder if it meant saving her daughter and using Evisceration on her own husband, on Calene's father, had only fed her lust for destruction. She hadn't intended it to happen that way, but when she woke, when she saw him standing over her...

She wondered if Arlo's father felt the same way about his son.

Zanna knelt down and met Arlo's eyes. "This is why we need to be vigilant. Why we need to find a better way. Evil tempts us. Power whispers to us, begs us to give in and take the easy path. Only there *is* no easy path. Just a price to be paid, sooner or later. We Sparkers have this inside us always, because the gods didn't give us a gift. They gave us a *responsibility*. Arlo, in that moment, my hatred, that darkness, felt alive, like I'd birthed it into the world. I fed it, made it strong, and in return it nearly consumed me. Do you understand?"

He nodded as tears ran down his cheeks. Zanna hugged him, her neck wet as he sobbed against her.

"How could someone experiment on their own child?" he whispered. "I understand why you did what you did, but...is it really that easy to fall? It just sounds so... wrong. Will they vote no, do you think?"

Zanna pulled away and wiped his face. "I don't know anymore," she admitted, getting to her feet. "Years ago, it wouldn't be a discussion. Now, it is and that scares me. Come on."

As they left the ramparts, colourful lights appeared in the skies above the Peaks of Eternity—shimmering greens and blues and reds, cascading and changing. The air shifted, just a touch, a stirring of the wind. Those watching on Solitude's walls Linked to tell those inside of the strange sight.

The Banished wailed and sank to their knees.

As they approached the dining hall, Zanna spotted Garet waiting by the doors. He gazed at the floor but looked up as they drew close.

"Zanna. A word."

"Go inside, Arlo," she told her apprentice. "I'll join you soon."

The boy scowled and slunk away into the hall, hands thrust inside his robes.

"Children," Garet said, shaking his head. "Full of wonder one second, a black mood the next."

"Some adults aren't so different, Garet," Zanna said. She walked across the corridor and took a seat in the reading area, signalling for the Protector to do the same. "Well? Talk."

Garet took a seat, expression dark, no doubt put out from her taking the lead. His chair screeched as he edged it closer. Their knees almost touched. She fought the urge to pull away.

"You must see what's at stake here," he said. Zanna could smell wine on his breath, saw it on his reddened cheeks. "We can hold them, funnel them in by altering the landscape so we can focus our defence in one area, but it'll only last so long. If we don't act, we grant them the initiative. Even if the vote goes my way, we can't afford to sit and do nothing. They could find a way to defeat us before we make our move. Who says they haven't already found it? We should have forced them away the moment they arrived. Our options are few now."

"Have you tried talking to them?" Zanna asked, tone placid.

"Pah!" Garet spat. "Have you lost your senses?"

"No. Actually, my senses are in agreement. The Banished are waiting for something. If they *wanted* to attack us, they'd do it. A small group waits near our walls. Their *leader* waits. It's a diplomatic party, Garet. They want to parley. Ride out to meet them."

Garet opened his mouth then closed it with a snap. He reminded Zanna of a fish. One with teeth and a nasty disposition.

"Impossible," he muttered. "Out of the question."

"Why?"

"We don't *meet* with the Banished," Garet snapped, the red in his cheeks turning purple. "Even if we did, I'd get more sense out of a droking elf. The last Sparker who made contact with them stated communication proved futile. Our languages are too different. Besides, why should *our* reaction be peaceful? Theirs is an act of aggression and should be met in kind. Solitude is mine to defend as I see fit. I won't yield, to you or them."

"If we don't meet them, we invite needless death and destruction."

Garet shot to his feet, eyes wide. He thrust a trembling finger in Zanna's face.

"It's you, and those who act against us taking the initiative, that invite death and destruction. Remember that."

He stalked into the dining hall. Zanna looked away.

A gong sounded from the dining room. The last of the Sparkers filed in. Zanna got to her feet and joined them, wishing she could shake the shiver that sank into her bones.

* * *

Sparkers dressed in bright yellows, greens, blues and purples milled around the dining hall, stepping forward one at a time to place their vote in the box, under the watchful eye of Protector Garet. He stared each of them in the eye as they approached and deposited their ballot, as if attempting to read or sway their minds. Almost all the Sparkers of Solitude filled the hall. Those on watch had cast their votes earlier in the day, sealing their envelope with a magic-infused wax seal. They would know when Garet unsealed the paper.

Zanna half-wished she could have cast her vote that way, instead of dropping it under the despot's watchful glare.

She waited her turn and strode to the box, matching his stare. She refused to be cowed by the likes of him.

"You of all people should know what's necessary," he said, as she stood before him. He seemed to hold her responsible for Solitude's dissenting voices. If he could alter her mind, the rest would follow suit.

"You're right," Zanna replied, dropping her vote into the box, "which is why I know it's necessary that no Sparker ever use Evisceration."

She spun on her heel and walked away, nodding to the next voter as she passed. Zanna took a seat on a bench next to Arlo, who sulked with his head resting on his arms on the table.

"I hate waiting," he muttered. He sat up and clicked his fingers, producing different coloured flames each time.

"That's Solitude," Zanna said, watching his magic. "Even the Banished are in on the act. Very nice, by the way."

"Thanks." He beamed at her. "You're not a bad teacher."

Zanna drew on her own energy, body heat lowering as if ice ran through her veins—her skin pricked from the coolness—and settled a shield around Arlo's hand, like an invisible bubble. Her temperature returned quickly to normal. Her student's eyes grew wide as he felt the magic touch his skin.

"Don't worry," Zanna smiled. "It's so you can practice in safety. You can expand this bubble as a shield to protect you from external attacks, too. Some Sparkers find it useful for drunken trips to the lavvy in the night. Try filling the shield with fire. It won't harm you; it comes from you."

Arlo frowned as he splayed his fingers. Different coloured flames spurted from his digits in a continuous gush. He held his hand in front of his face and laughed.

"Amazing," he said, waving his fire-hand from side-to-side, multi-coloured lights flickering off the robes of the nearby Sparkers.

"You're drawing a crowd, maestro." Zanna pointed

around the room. Several Sparkers looked at the lesson in progress, a fun distraction from the drudgery of the voting. "But remember that this isn't just a pretty trick. It can be dangerous, too. If I removed the shield, you'd burn us all down, and this is just from the magic inside you. Imagine if you borrowed energy from elsewhere."

The flames dwindled and went out. Arlo wriggled his fingers as he examined them.

"Tired?"

"No," he said in a thoughtful tone. "Not even a little."

Zanna raised her eyebrows and measured his power. *It's grown in the last week,* she thought, *more than it should.*

Guilt prodded at her. Between the Banished and the possibility of Calene entering her life again, she'd been neglecting Arlo.

"Your power could outstrip us all, Arlo," she said, shaking her head. "I hope I teach you the correct way to use it."

"I hope so, too," the boy replied, a faraway look in his bright eyes. "Something's nagging at me, Master. Not quite fear."

"There's enough people to fill three cities at our gates. You're worried about the Banished. It's natural. I can't pretend I'm not worried too."

Arlo paused and closed his eyes, as if he sought to order his thoughts before speaking.

"No," he muttered at last, shaking his head. "It's not them. At least, not all about them. You know I hear their singing in my sleep, too? When I'm dreaming. Do you hear them?"

"No," Zanna said, relieved her apprentice broached his nightmares at last, "but I'm not surprised the Banished are in your dreams."

"I'm frightened of this Spark inside me," Arlo went on. "It's such a beautiful thing but...terrible too. Now they want us to become even more like weapons... I don't want that."

Zanna laid a hand on his shoulder and looked him in the eye. *If only you made the decisions around here,* she thought, proud of her apprentice's innocence.

"It's your choice. No one can force you. The Spark is yours, and so are your decisions. Live by them."

Could she really give that advice? Her decision, ten years before, had cost her everything. Her position, her home, her daughter.

Have I lived by them? she thought. *Or have I hid myself away at the end of the world and let them consume me?*

Arlo frowned at his hands, and Zanna took the chance to glance at Garet as he counted the votes. Two piles of paper grew in front of him as he placed the ballots on the table, though one stack soon outstripped the other. Zanna studied his impassive face, searching for a sign. Which way would the decision go?

"Can we talk about my dreams, Zanna?"

She turned to him. He peered at her, eyes filled with fear. It struck her then; his refusal to talk about his nightmares didn't stem from some boyish notion of strength. Even the *idea* of talking about them petrified him.

"Of course. Now?"

"Later," Arlo replied, his bottom lip trembling. "After the vote."

Conversations around the hall drifted into silence as the Sparkers watched their leader. The quiet amplified the Banished's singing and the music filled the cavernous walls. They felt closer than before as they waited in nervous stillness.

Placing one last piece of paper down with deliberate care, Garet climbed to his feet.

"An outcome. A verdict has reached a majority of one-hundred-and-one votes, so I won't count the rest," he said, without amplifying his voice. Zanna leaned forward to hear. "Solitude's Sparkers have voted to reject the Council's directive."

He fell silent, gaze lingering on each assembled Sparker before it fell on Zanna.

"I only asked that you give me the means to be proactive, to fight to our full potential, and spare those innocent souls in Adhraas that will suffer the wrath of the Banished when they sweep beyond Solitude. There is an army at our walls, and they won't hesitate when the time comes. Mark my words; I guarantee you, this vote has doomed us all."

Garet swept out of the hall, leaving a stunned silence in his wake. Zanna looked around at the others. None appeared pleased with the outcome. The gravity of their situation weighed heavy. Some got to their feet, shaking their heads and followed Garet from the room.

"What does this mean?" Arlo whispered, tugging at Zanna's sleeve. For reasons she couldn't fathom, many of the remaining Sparkers were looking to her now.

"It means we must find another way of keeping the Banished where they are." She winked at him, an attempt to put him at ease despite her dread. "There's always another way."

Zanna returned to her rooms alone. Arlo insisted on delving further in the library, and she allowed him the opportunity to distract himself. She wanted to speak to him of his dreams, like he'd asked, but for the moment the issue seemed forgotten.

She wandered to the ramparts above the gigantic main gate that led out onto the plains beyond Solitude. She paused at a window overlooking the forest trail that led towards the fringes of Haltveldt's territories.

How long since I've stared this way?

The night's frost dusted the grass either side of the road leading from Solitude into Adhraas village and the harbour, ten miles south. Some of her fellow Sparkers journeyed there on occasion. She never had.

She'd last visited the place ten years earlier, when her exile began. She hadn't left Solitude since. She'd immersed herself in her new life and spared little thought of the outside world, seeking to rid herself of the memories that haunted her, that assaulted her when she closed her eyes, no matter how much she studied, working until her bones screamed with weariness.

Months passed, and Zanna attempted contact with her daughter. Calene's resentment, her disgust, had struck her like a physical blow and she'd retreated into herself. She kept to her rooms, and haunted the corridors of Solitude, alone and silent, even pulling away from Miriam's friendship for a time.

During that time, Solitude had truly been her prison, but one she'd created for herself. The idea of journeying to Adhraas frightened her. What if the people there discovered her crimes? What would they do to the woman who had given in to her darkness and Eviscerated her own husband?

As the years ticked by, the fortress's tall walls and icy rooms became her world. She'd lived a decade in Solitude's shadow.

She resumed her climb to the stronghold's highest point. The people of Adhraas would bear the brunt of their failure to defend Solitude. The town's leaders believed the Banished posed no threat and wouldn't order an evacuation. If the attack came, it would be a massacre.

Zanna tested her connection with Calene again, edging into it, and sighed when she felt the barrier once more.

Have we done the right thing here? Holding to the Laws? She cast the words towards her daughter, though she knew Calene wouldn't hear them. *You'd say yes. I know you would. The world isn't black and white though, and we're naïve if we expect to live that way.*

She thought of Arlo, and how he feared the Spark inside him. Calene had feared Zanna, when she woke and discovered the remains of her father. She had scared herself. Still did. The thought that her instinct had been something so terrible, that the power had spilled out of her without a thought of another way, chilled her. Now, she *knew* there'd been a better way, but she feared, if put in the same position again, she'd do the same thing.

For her daughter. For Arlo.

Maybe we're not so different after all, Garet.

Bells rang from the watchtowers, snapping her from the dark corners of her mind. Zanna ran.

She reached the top of the tallest tower and gasped, raising her hand to her mouth in shock. The skies above the Peaks of Eternity writhed in a kaleidoscope of colour, the shades mixing and warping as they blended together.

A shrill wail pierced the air. Ignoring the other Sparkers keeping watch on the rampart, Zanna fumbled for the telescope at her hip and scanned the Banished. They faced the mountains, some on their knees, others with arms stretched towards the skies, screaming as one. Their howls drove daggers into Zanna's heart; their lament carried so much pain and loss.

She turned the telescope to the party of Banished who'd approached the walls the day before. The riders pelted back to their ranks, leaving the leader alone. The man stood with his arms open wide, shouting up at them.

To Zanna's eyes, it seemed he looked at her, pleading with her.

Thunder rumbled in the distance. More than that, it sounded like the sky itself began to tear apart. The lights grew more violent, pulsating and swirling faster than before. The Banished wailed, and the thunder rumbled louder, the heavens roaring fury at the earth. Zanna sank to her knees and the other Sparkers followed, gritting teeth and pressing hands to their ears as the cacophony threatened to overwhelm them.

Then, just as Zanna feared her head would explode from the chaos, the furious roar from the sky faded. The Banished fell silent with it. Zanna blinked and glanced around.

She struggled to her feet, rubbing the pressure from her temples and accessed her Second Sight. Along the ramparts, Zanna saw other Sparkers doing the same.

A mighty shield—a shimmering, translucent blue—covered the walls in a dome, protecting Solitude from the shale at its foot to the pinnacle of its tallest tower. The sound hadn't disappeared; something had shut it out instead. The lights still battled each other for dominance in the sky, reflecting on the surface of the globe and spreading their changing light across Solitude.

Her panic turned to calm as she watched Sparkers flood the walls from below—led by Garet, of all people—merging their Spark to build the barrier of magic over Solitude. It wouldn't halt physical attacks, her Sight told her that, but it *would* protect against magic. Common knowledge told them the Banished didn't possess any power but something had caused the cacophony raging above the Peaks of Eternity. If not them, what?

She gazed out and watched the Banished scream into

the skies, their cries dulled by the barrier. The riders had reached the front lines and rallied them. Beyond the magical shield, horns sounded and weapons rattled as soldiers marched to join the lone man ahead of them.

"Master?"

Zanna spun. Arlo stood behind her, pointing into the sky. His thin arm trembled as the lights from the heavens reflected in his eyes. She closed the gap to him, and drew him close. He wept against her chest, body shaking.

"There now," she murmured, watching the lights swirl above the monstrous mountains on the horizon. "You're safe here with me."

"No," Arlo managed, through his tears. "None of us are safe. I dreamt of this. The sky tearing itself apart. A bright green wave of light sweeps down from the mountains and crashes into Solitude. The Banished scream, they wail, they cry as they flood the walls. A shadow waits, in my mind, in my dreams. It comes for us all, Master, and there's nothing we can do. Nothing!"

He fell, sobbing, into her arms. She laid a hand against his back, and felt it rise as he breathed.

Their waiting is over, Zanna thought, a tear falling down her cheek as she held her apprentice tight. *The defence of Solitude begins. Raas save us all.*

CHAPTER NINE
THE UNEXPECTED

'Avastia? I've seen it. Two monarchs—one human, one elf. Place is dreary, wet, and full of secrets.' - Heron, a renowned explorer.

"**W**ake up."

The words stirred her from sleep. A slap did the rest.

Calene snapped upright in the mud. She remembered Vettigan, the Shadow Sparker's attack. She *definitely* remembered Zal's knee. Then the stallion, trampling its rider into the dirt, the sound of bones snapping. The *silence* even as she struck the thing over and over again, until the very moment its head left its body.

How did it get up after that? she thought, her hand straying towards the sword on her hip. *Did I pass out?*

Calene gazed around. The Banished sat in the back of the cart, staring at the prone body of Vettigan. She wanted to run to him, check on her friend. If she could see the damage herself, maybe she could try to fix it.

The elf crouched in front of her, hands slick with

blood. She nodded at Calene.

"I moved the bodies, but we should leave soon," she said, wiping a hand on her cloak and holding it out.

Calene hesitated, then gripped it. The elf pulled her to her feet with ease, as if she were a child. Tall and lithe, her bright red hair framed tanned, freckled skin and green eyes. Beneath the dirty green cloak, she clad herself in dark leather armour, well-worn and regularly patched. The mantle of a seasoned fighter, one who relied on speed and natural grace.

"I put them in a pit and burned them. Just in case they were thinking of getting up again."

Calene suppressed a shiver. *That Shadow Sparker... There's more of them.*

She eyed the elf. "*We* should leave? Don't elves kill Sparkers on sight?"

"Why? Would you like me to kill you?" She gazed over at the cart, seeming bored. "Seems like it would be too easy, in your current state. And a waste of an opportunity for me. Travelling with humans would make my life a little easier this far north. Why not feed me, and I'll travel with you awhile?"

"Raas' teeth, the beggar playing the sellsword now? Rubbish." Calene stood between the elf and the cart, arms folded. "You didn't just happen upon that ambush. You've been watching us the whole time, since we met you on the road back there. Why? What does an elf want with two travellers and a mule? Unless it's not us at all. I saw you looking at our friend back on the road. Now you can't take your eyes off him. What is he to you?"

The elf narrowed her eyes and chewed her bottom lip.

"I'm not sure. Can't describe it. Your kind wouldn't understand, I suspect. My eyes tell me he's what you call Banished." She smiled and poked Calene in the chest. "That picture in your cloak was interesting though. I know what *that* is. Do you?"

"Why don't you tell me?" Calene snapped, fighting back a flash of annoyance from the thought of the elf rummaging through her pockets.

"On the road," the elf replied, scooping the water skin that Calene gave her from her cloak and pouring it over her hands to wash away the blood.

"Get droked. You think I'll take you on your word? Teeth of the gods, woman."

"Believe what you will," the elf said, with a shrug. "I didn't need to rescue you."

Irritated as it made Calene to admit, she was right. The other woman could have stolen the cart; all their belongings, too. She'd been the last one standing after the battle.

She spat on the ground, anger bubbling up inside her.

Relax. You're not annoyed at the elf. Your own droking kind attacked you. You just got Eviscerated, they nearly killed Vettigan and you found out they've had Sparkers like that *the whole time. She's the only one you* know *is on your side.*

"Fine," Calene said. "What's your name?"

"Brina," the elf replied. She tossed her thin bag into the back of the cart.

"Right." Calene stalked to the rear of the cart. "Can you check the Sparkers' horses for anything we can use while I see to the men?"

She didn't wait to see if Brina followed her commands. She needed to help Vettigan and she'd already wasted too much time. The state she found him in sank stones to the pit of her stomach.

Her friend had caught up with his age, looking every day of his almost one hundred and eight years. His luscious, grey locks had thinned and turned white; in some places, they had fallen out and left patches of baldness, scalp dotted with liver spots. His frame had gone beyond thin to emaciated, his skin grey-hued and wrinkled. His eyes, no longer bright, stared unblinking into the twilight skies. If it wasn't for the shuddering breaths he sucked in, Calene would have thought him dead.

Ganton's Evisceration had brushed her and she still felt weary from it, head still throbbing. The Shadow Sparker had Vettigan in its clutches for longer, and the black miasma she'd seen forcing its way into her friend's body with her Second Sight... She'd never seen anything like it before.

She glanced at the Banished. He peered back at her, yellow eyes solemn but focused, looking no worse for wear after his brush with Zal. Calene hadn't forgotten the puzzle he represented; Evisceration had faltered when it touched him. She knew magic could affect him—she'd healed him days before—but the most powerful, and most vile, weapon a Sparker could wield couldn't touch him.

The Empire's Sparkers, Calene thought, a chill running down her spine. *Just wait till they find out we have an elf, too. Drok, we can't trust anyone. We're outlaws in our own nation.*

"Vettigan," she muttered, laying her palm against his chest, "you poor fool. I'll do what I can."

She closed her eyes and opened herself to the surrounding world. She drank in the energies of the water dripping from the leaves, the wind whispering in her ears, the last rays of sunlight licking the sky. Calene pulled it all into her and more. She discovered flames devouring the bodies of the Shadow Sparker, Ganton and Zal in a pit dug by the elf. She let the energies build inside her, felt her weariness evaporate, the pain in her face fade.

Calene wanted to hold on, to absorb it, to let it mend and strengthen her. Then she wanted *more.* A Sparker's curse. She drew a little more, approaching what she could safely hold, then jerked as she felt another presence.

Something unique.

The Banished sang, so soft, so tender. A wordless tune that pulsated with energy. She almost lost control of her focus, but she drew that in too. It felt sweeter than life itself. Innocent and pure.

Calene quivered with the Spark. Life flowed within her, bolstered by the Banished's song. She held more raw magic than she'd ever tried to contain before. Something told her she could gather more, push further, with the Banished's tune empowering her, but now wasn't the moment to experiment.

She let the energies flow into her arm, her skin smouldering with fire, prickling with frost, then released it through her palm and into Vettigan's chest. She pictured him the way he'd appeared before—the man she'd known all her life, who'd taken her under his wing after her father's betrayal and her mother's exile. The man who'd stood by her as she dealt with the grief, the anger. Her body shook as she forced her Spark into him, thoughts drifting to the content look on his face when they'd sit by a fire, drinking, talking long into the night and watching the sun rise together. The Sparker, her friend, larger than several lives.

No, more than her friend. Her family.

Come back to me, Vettigan. Please...

The magic enveloped him...but something inside him swallowed it. Calene opened her Second Sight and saw the shadow writhing beneath his skin, like a parasite feeding, alive and moving. A taint left by the Shadow Sparker's Evisceration. With a shudder, she recalled seeing it forcing its way into his body and realised it lingered still.

She pushed more into him, including her own life energy. Sweat broke out in beads across her brow and still she worked, even though her body grew cold and her vision blurred. Blood trickled from her nose, ears and the corners of her eyes, and she grit her teeth, lips curled back.

More, she thought, muscles burning, cramping. *Raas' teeth, he needs more.*

Calene approached her limits, she knew it, but the darkness had defeated her. Vettigan would die. The dark magic used against him still worked inside, and would continue until it fed on every morsel of energy inside his body.

"No," she breathed, thoughts coming slow, shivers running up and down her spine. "You can't droking have him. I won't let you take him from me."

She felt a firm hand grip her forearm. The sudden bloom of heat felt scalding. Calene looked up, meeting the Banished's smiling, yellow eyes.

"Mi sineh ovren cha," he said, glancing at Vettigan. With care, he lifted Calene's hand away. She tried to fight him off, but strength had left her. She may as well have been trying to mould iron with her bare hands.

"What?" she gasped, releasing the energy. The world dimmed and spun. She'd have fallen if the Banished hadn't held her.

"Mi sineh ovren cha," he repeated, voice rich and vibrant.

He smiled at her and placed his fingertips to Vettigan's forehead. The Banished chanted in a low, melodious tone. Through her Second Sight, Calene could see the shadow inside Vettigan writhe and shrink and, even as she listened, she felt strength flood her body once more, like the song nourished her.

"By the gods," she whispered, leaning forward to study Vettigan closer. "It's working. How?"

She watched as the shadow parasite continued to dissipate, until only a blemish the size of her thumb lay above Vettigan's brain. To Calene's eyes, a bright light surrounded it, as if the Banished had contained it with his chanting and ringed the shadow in.

Like Solitude and the Peaks of Eternity, Calene thought, *surrounding the Banished.*

Even if the darkness remained, his body might now be able to heal. She tried again, releasing only a trickle this time, and gasping as her Spark responded. Between the ambush and her last attempt at healing, she knew she should have been on the verge of burning out, but the song made everything easier. Connections broader and deeper, magic flowing like water from the world into her. And from her into Vettigan. His body devoured her Spark, feeding on it, limbs trembling in response.

"Thank you!" She beamed at the Banished. The pale man smiled back, encouraging her with his hands as he chanted, voice a higher pitch than before.

Calene sent more energy into Vettigan's body as Brina climbed into the cart, hood pulled over her face. She noticed the elf's eyes flicking to the Banished as his song ended.

"He's looking better," she said, gazing down at the stricken man.

Calene nodded. Some wrinkles had faded, and colour returned to his flesh, but the ordeal had left its mark. His eyes were hooded, features sallow, jowls drooping from his cheekbones. She stopped and leaned back, knowing somehow that she'd done all she could.

The shadow still sat on Vettigan's brain, hemmed in by whatever the Banished had done. Calene knew he needed more than she could provide. She knew of only one person more accomplished at healing than her—Zanna. If anyone could do it, her mother could.

Calene sat back and glanced at the Banished, brain and body tired as she tried to order her thoughts. He gazed back, the fading light passing through the trees dancing in his eyes.

"Where to?" Brina asked, taking the mule's reins.

"We can't go to Spring Haven," she said, covering Vettigan with a blanket. "Colton is by the sea; it has a port. We'll head there, take a boat to Solitude. It's far away from the capital and it means we can avoid the Imperial Highway. They may know something about our 'friend' that I don't. And my mother is there."

Calene ignored Brina's grimace at the mention of Colton, and left out the news of the Banished mustering at Solitude's gates. She thought she could help. Or maybe their strange companion could, if they returned him unharmed. She didn't want to reflect on her decision to head towards her mother, how her first thoughts when in trouble, with Vettigan incapacitated, went to Zanna.

Raas' teeth. I'll stick my fingers into that old wound another time. Why not? It's for Vettigan, after all.

She needed answers, and the encounter with the Sparkers told her they weren't safe in Haltveldt. A war brewed on Solitude's doorstep, but perhaps she and her strange companion held the key to halting it.

"Solitude harran va liesh!" the Banished crowed, clapping his hands.

"Well, at least someone's droking happy," Calene muttered.

"Liesh?" Brina said, turning in her seat.

He nodded. "Liesh."

"You understand what he's saying?" Calene said, staring between them.

"Not everything," Brina said, after a pregnant pause. "But 'liesh' is an elvish word. It means 'purpose.'"

Calene looked at the Banished, and he smiled back.

"Solitude," he said in his musical voice. He pointed at himself, then Brina and held up one more finger. "Ila braun."

"Right," Calene replied, climbing into the driver's seat. Brina's features settled into a frown. "That's settled it. Solitude it is, unless anyone has a better idea? Let's get a droking move on."

"Stop looking at him," Calene grumbled, glancing at the elf beside her. Brina kept swivelling in the cart to glance at the Banished, who in turn watched the sleeping Vettigan.

"Fine," the redhead replied, and turned her emerald-eyed stare on Calene instead.

"Don't do that, either."

"What would make you more comfortable? Should I watch the skies and the trees?"

"I don't—" Calene began, then bit her lip and sighed. "Sorry. I should be thanking you. I'm just worried for Vettigan. My own people tried to kill me and that Shadow

Sparker? It's thrown me a little off-balance, that's all. Sitting next to you like we're Raas and Janna heading to Eru on prayer day doesn't help, either."

The cart's wheels creaked as they passed through the Forest of Mists towards Colton, daylight fading, the mule's hooves muffled by the mud on the ground. She felt it best not to mention her mother, or the sinking feeling she got every time her thoughts turned to Solitude. Brina laid a hand on Calene's forearm. The Sparker felt the calluses against her skin, but didn't pull away.

She looked up to see the other woman's eyes fixed on her, bright and piercing. Calene studied her face and saw beauty beneath the fine scars crisscrossing her features. She coughed and looked away.

"Tell me about yourself," she said, and stared intently into the woods so Brina wouldn't notice the heat rising in her cheeks. The woman's eyes unnerved her. Or maybe her lips. "Just Brina, is it?"

She felt the elf shift in her seat and scowled. Staring at the Banished again.

"Brina al'Loria," she answered. Calene enjoyed the melody of elvish spoken by a native tongue.

"You're familiar with this duchy?"

"I've travelled. Familiar with a lot of places. Been as far as Gallavan's Seat and all the way down to the Widows."

Calene gave her a sidelong look. "You know Colton well, is what I mean. That's plain enough. I noticed your little grimace when I mentioned the place earlier."

Brina frowned and flicked her fingers at unseen bugs

hovering in the surrounding air.

"I've...dealt with the traders there. Once or twice. I don't enjoy returning to this area. My family once owned land in these parts, before the Empire came."

Calene did a double-take. Colton, and the lands around it, had been a part of the Hiberian Duchy, the last to hold out against Haltveldt's expansion. Hiberia itself had been levelled in the final battle when the siege broke. Sharing a border with the elves, the people in these parts had enjoyed close ties with their neighbours. They'd resisted the Empire's anti-elven propaganda more fiercely than most.

But two centuries had passed since Haltveldt absorbed Colton and the Hiberian Duchy.

"How old are you?" Calene asked.

"I stopped counting at three hundred," Brina muttered, sniffing the air. She appeared distracted, though Calene conceded she'd made the elf uncomfortable with her questions.

"Raas' teeth," Calene laughed, attempting to lighten the mood. "You don't look a day over one hundred and fifty."

Instead of smiling, Brina held up a hand. Stop. Calene's heart sank. Gifted with the Spark and the sword, certainly, but never with the hearts of women.

They approached a crossroad, and the elf's eyes narrowed as she peered around.

"Stop the cart."

"No," Calene objected. "We're in a hurry and—"

"I said," Brina bit out. "Stop. The. Cart."

The edge in her voice made Calene act. She sawed the reigns, bringing the mule to an abrupt halt. Birds twittered in the late-afternoon sky, and the wind rustled through the leaves of the trees. She couldn't tell what had Brina so spooked she'd reached for her sword under her cloak.

"What is it?"

"Listen," Brina whispered, pointing to the road to their right. "Chains. Slavers approaching."

"Slavers?" Calene strained her hearing. Seconds passed before she heard it, the clink of metal against metal. "That means... Drok. They only keep one kind of people as slaves."

Brina ignored her, staring down the road towards the noises. That confirmed it.

"Oi," Calene hissed, twisting in her seat to glare at the Banished. He sat beside Vettigan, bold as daylight, smiling back at her. She mimed lifting a hood. "Keep covered. Don't so much as breathe too loud, got it?" She turned to Brina. The elf reminded her of a coiled viper. "Same goes for you. We don't want more trouble."

The rattle of chains grew louder, as did the clatter of hooves, and still Brina hadn't moved an inch.

"Raas' teeth, woman," Calene growled, gathering her Spark. "Pull up your hood or I'll do it myself."

Brina's eyes flicked to hers for a moment and her face softened. Nodding, she drew up her hood and slumped in her seat. Calene urged the mule on, but drew it to a stop when the slaving party came into sight.

Don't stop. Don't try to talk to us. Just keep droking moving.

"Let the filth rest a moment," a heavyset man at the caravan's head shouted over his shoulder.

Drok…

He turned to look at Calene, taking in her party without a word. She returned the favour. Two men on horseback rode behind him—mercenaries, judging by the swords and bows strapped to their backs. A row of twelve chained elves sagged to the floor behind them. Mostly children, some as young as four or five. Two more mounted fighting men brought up the rear.

"What news, travellers?" the leader greeted. "Name's Tark. I'm heading for Colton."

Calene felt Brina tense beside her and fought the urge to place a hand on her sword arm.

"I'm Zanty," she lied, with a nonchalant shrug. Or at least, she hoped it looked that way.

She considered her own small party—hoods up and heads down—from the slavers' perspective, and knew how odd they looked. Better than thinking about the elven-children, emaciated and chained. The anger coiled in her and her Spark grew, unbidden. She smothered the sparks growing on her fingertips in her damp cloak.

"A simple merchant, travelling from Temek," she said. "This is my sister Zara, and my brother Huw. Mute, I'm afraid. My father's in the back with him. Armed men robbed us on the road a while back and he took a nasty turn. Hoping to find help in Colton."

Tark nodded and threw a thumb over his shoulder at his swellswords. If it came to it, Calene reckoned she could incapacitate them all with her Spark, but her magic would stand out like a beacon for any other Sparkers watching the roads. After their encounter with the Shadow Sparker, Ganton and Zal, she couldn't rule it out. There'd be more. A secret that threatened Haltveldt rode in her cart and the Emperor wouldn't have sent just one party to retrieve it. Sparkers could sense magic at a distance. The amount needed to fight them would stand out like a bonfire in the night.

Tark spat. "Bandits all over in these parts. Need a few fighters to protect your wares."

"Is that what they are?" Brina's voice curled out of her lips in a hiss that carried through the crossroads. "Wares?"

"Elven scum, is what they are," Tark laughed. "Bought them from an Empire raiding party, reckon I can turn a pretty profit selling them to the nobles in Spring Haven. They like 'em young and female."

Calene pressed her foot down on Brina's. This time, she *did* put a hand on her sword arm.

"We'll accompany you on the road to Colton," Tark offered. "It's only a few miles, and I couldn't sleep if I heard you ran afoul of any more bandits. I'm a good citizen, after all."

Drok, Calene thought, gritting her teeth, *of all the things for Raas to set on our path. A community-minded slaver. Rot your droking teeth!*

"Thank you," she called, and bowed her head. "After you, kind sir."

Tark signalled for the caravan to move on and Calene's heart tried to escape from her mouth.

As the chained elves stumbled forwards, a child second-in-line fell into the elf in front. The entire line crashed to the ground in a mess of mud and limbs. The children's cries of fear, pain, and misery knifed Calene between the ribs.

"Mazlet," Tark shouted, with a scowl. "Get them on their feet, will you? Useless filth."

One fighter leapt down from his horse and dragged the offending child to her feet. Calene watched, fingers itching to Spark, as the guard towered over the girl. Even from her distance, Calene could see the fear in the little one's wide eyes.

"Thought you droking elves were supposed to be graceful," Mazlet growled, grabbing the child by the front of her rags. "Could have damaged the whole of the boss's stock with your clumsiness. I'll teach you to watch your step."

His gauntleted hand struck the girl across the face, sending her sprawling into the mud. Mazlet stooped to grab her again, and Calene realised Brina had left the cart.

Her eyes blazed, her hood fell back, her braided red hair spilled in her wake, and before anyone could shout the word 'elf', her thin, curved blade removed Mazlet's head in one clean slice. A wordless cry of rage tore from her throat as the headless body toppled.

It fell on top of the shocked elf-child, pinning her to the ground, and the crossroad held its breath.

"What are you waiting for?" Tark cried, spittle flying from his lips. "Kill 'em all!"

Steel rang as the mercenaries drew their weapons and sprang into action.

The Banished roared, almost knocking Calene from her seat as he leapt from the cart and threw himself into the fray, broadsword raised. He barged a man to the ground with his shoulder as Brina turned to meet the blade of another.

"Drok it," Calene snarled, hopping down from the driver's seat and drawing her longsword.

She charged at a third mercenary closing in on Brina, already engaged, teeth bared and eyes alive with fury.

The Banished had dispatched one of the guardsmen already with a clean thrust through the chest and now stood in front of the line of chained elves. Tark glared at him from atop his horse, a mace clutched in his hand. Doubt flickered on his face as he deliberated on which would prove more valuable: his stock or his life.

Calene intercepted the sword meant for Brina, arm vibrating with the impact. She heard a body drop beside her and prayed it wasn't Brina's but knew looking would spell doom. Her opponent attacked with intent, swinging high and low with speed and skill.

Damn you, Raas, she snarled, defending herself as best she could. *I'd have to get the only one with any talent.*

Calene heard a clatter of hooves and a horse scream, and her attacker's eyes shifted behind her for just a moment.

"Last mistake you'll make, friend," she crowed.

Calene lunged high, and the mercenary twisted his blade to defend a fraction too late. Her sword slid across his and she ducked, letting go of the hilt. She spun and caught the falling sword in a reverse grip, driving it through the mercenary's stomach. Blood poured from his mouth as Calene pulled her sword free.

I've killed a man, Calene thought, staring into his face as it twisted with pain. *Over an elf. I didn't even think about it. But it's right, damn it! I know it is!*

He dropped to his knees, and she swung once more. His head toppled to the floor. A quick death.

"Better than dying from steel to the gut," Calene muttered, spinning on the spot. "Better than you deserve."

Brina still lived, as did the Banished. The elf straddled Tark. She had driven her blade through his chest, pinning him to the ground.

"Look at me," Brina hissed, face inches from the slaver's nose. "I want you to see me as you die and know an elf killed you. Your 'wares' will walk free again and you... You're going to learn that this is the price of your greed."

She seized his jaw, holding his agonised screaming in as he gouged furrows in the dirt with his heels. He still struggled when Calene couldn't watch anymore and pretended to check on Vettigan again. It took him agonising minutes to expire and, by then, the elves had helped pull the fallen girl to her feet and stood, staring at them.

Finally, Brina got to her feet and pulled her sword free, blood spreading across the trail. She didn't bother to close his eyes.

"Nice little fight, that," she muttered, refusing to meet Calene's eyes.

"Nice little fight?" she spat. She pointed at the chained elves. "What the drok are we meant to do with them? It's going to be hard enough to get a Raas-forsaken ship to take us up to Solitude with *one* elf in tow, let alone *thirteen*."

She heard the clang of metal and shouts of surprise. Glancing over her shoulder, she saw the Banished hammering at the chains with his mighty broadsword, freeing each slave in turn.

Brina scowled. "Look, I don't expect you to understand—"

"Are you insane?" Calene cried, slamming her sword into its sheath and throwing up her hands. "Of course I understand. These are your people. Drok, even *I* wanted to act when that fool struck the girl. I've no love for slavers but, teeth of the gods, we're outlaws already. What are we going to do? Liberate the entire area of every elf we come across, lead an uprising and sail our merry way north? We need to get to Solitude, Brina. Before it's too late."

Brina glanced at the elves. They huddled together, some sobbing, others staring at the Banished with a mixture of gratitude, fear and wonder. The strange warrior grinned back at them.

"Listen, I know some folk in Colton. Smugglers. They'll help. I've...used them before."

Calene raised her eyebrows and breathed through her nose. Brina gave a small shrug and added an almost embarrassed smile.

"Someday, you're going to tell me all about your life, Brina," she muttered. "Alright, smuggle them where?"

"Avastia. Let me go on ahead with them, off the road. I'll meet up with you in Colton." She glanced at her kin again, pity and desperation etched in her face. "Please."

"Fine," Calene grumbled. Gratitude from Brina, clear as day. "But if I don't get Vettigan to Solitude quickly... The only person who can help him is there. And the Banished might be our best chance to stop another war. I can't wait for you. If you're there, you can come along. If not... Then I guess this is goodbye."

Brina nodded and gripped Calene's shoulder. She ignored the urge to take the elf's hand when she pulled away. Brina marched towards the elves, speaking their language in a commanding voice. Within moments, they had faded into the surrounding trees, leaving Calene alone with the Banished, the unconscious Vettigan and a bunch of dead slavers. The Banished pointed at them, a quizzical look on his face.

"Leave 'em," Calene replied with a sigh. "Like Tark said, there're bandits everywhere. We'll hide the chains."

The strange warrior let out a musical laugh as he returned to the cart. Calene stayed, peering into the forest, hoping it wasn't the last she'd seen of Brina.

⁃——◇——⁃

Calene smiled as she saw the elf waiting for them on the approach to town, but smothered her relief out with a quick cough. Brina hopped into the cart without a word, face like stone. Calene knew better than to ask any questions. She figured they could wait for another time.

Their time in Colton went without further incident. A small port town that thrived on the businesses of the sea, which meant the place had its fair share of smugglers and privateers and no one looked for trouble unless they were trying to avoid it. Calene made her way to the docks alone to secure them passage, spinning a story about taking her grandfather to Solitude for healing.

"Those Sparkers up north work cheaper than the bastards in Spring Haven," the shipmaster agreed, and asked no further questions.

Brina and the Banished remained cloaked and silent as they brought Vettigan in. Calene arranged the sale of the mule and cart to buy their passage.

She spent all the money she had on the next available boat to Solitude, and even paid extra to make sure there would be no other stops. A four-day sail. If she used her Spark to direct the wind, they might make it in three.

The money only went so far, securing them one small cabin to share. Vettigan slept on the single bed built into the hull, still recovering from his ordeal. Calene used her Second Sight to peer at him; whatever the Banished had done continued to work. The shadow parasite left behind from the failed Evisceration lingered, contained within the Banished's shield of light. That it sat on Vettigan's brain concerned Calene, but still she marvelled at what the pale warrior's song had achieved.

The Banished and Brina sat in silent contemplation, facing each other. The elf seemed deep in thought, but their strange companion smiled away at her, cheerful as ever, but maybe with a hint of relief now.

Calene closed her eyes and reached out with her senses. She manipulated the winds, urging them to lift the waves and push the boat along Haltveldt's coast, keeping its sails taut. When she'd first learned to do it, she'd needed to be out in the open, to see the sky. These days, she could have done it five miles underground if she'd wanted.

Satisfied, she relaxed, releasing the maelstrom of energy swirling through her body and sighed as she did. Releasing the Spark always made her feel so empty. Diminished. Still, the work she did with the weather impressed even her.

Maybe we'll make Solitude in two-and-a-half days. I hope mother is okay.

Zanna hadn't contacted her since... Since just before the Shadow Sparker attack. Since Calene had *blocked* their Link.

Raas' rotten droking teeth, I am such an idiot.

She lowered her walls and pushed against the part of her mind where their Link resided.

Gods, I'm sorry, mother. Vettigan and I, we were attack by droking Sparkers on the road. Listen, the Empire has a new weapon. They've repealed the Laws of Engagement but it's worse than that. They have Sparkers who must have been using Evisceration for months, maybe years. They called it a Shadow Sparker. It...

She hesitated before she could tell her mother about Vettigan, about Brina and the slavers. She could sense her, but she didn't respond. Something had happened in Solitude and whatever it was demanded every ounce of concentration Zanna had.

Drok, she thought. *Not good. I really do hope she's okay. Maybe I should have told her that, come to think of it.*

Calene turned her attention to Brina, studying the scars that ran across her cheeks, the hard plains of her face. She understood her reaction at seeing her kind chained, treated like animals, but the way she'd killed the slaver, Tark, the way she'd watched him die...

It felt personal, like she'd relived some trauma in that moment.

"Hey," she said, nudging Brina with her foot. "About time you answered some questions, I reckon."

The other woman looked up and blinked at her, as if falling back into herself from the recesses of her mind.

"Fine," she said. "What do you want to know?"

"We could start with how you're familiar with Avastian smugglers." The boat swayed. Calene took a pull from her water skin and tried to push the seasickness away. "Or how about where you came from? Why you were sitting at the roadside in the Forest of Mists? How you got past the elven frontline without being in chains? How you've managed to evade capture so long in Imperial lands? Stop me if you hear a question you like the sound of."

"How much do you know about elves?"

"You mean, from before you were slaves, living in

slums and chased by armies? Just what they tell us at the University, and what they told us before that in school. They told us you're sub-human. Animals. Untrustworthy traitors who turned on humans after we forced the Banished north." She paused, meeting Brina's iron glare. "From my knowledge, I know your kind and the Empire descended into open war centuries ago, and you've fought alone since Haltveldt absorbed your allies, one-by-one. That your kind are used as slaves, forced to live in slums unless you live in the elven territories, and even then your days are numbered because the Empire's war machine won't stop until you're a memory. And I know you're fierce in battle because I've seen elves fell men from three hundred paces with a single arrow and your Sparkers rip the lives out of soldiers by the dozen."

"We're fighting for our lives," Brina said, heat rising in her voice. "We're all that stands between an army of butchers and innocent families who can't protect themselves. What do you expect us to do?"

"Right," Calene said, spreading her hands. "But that's not the point. You asked. I serve the gods, for all the good it does. I never wanted any part of genocide and slavery and I still don't. Remember, I helped you on the road to Colton, but those men weren't criminals. Not in Imperial lands. And I've watched friends torn apart and Eviscerated to nothing by your mages."

"War makes criminals of us all," Brina muttered. She looked at the Banished, who smiled back at her, as though they weren't even having an argument. "The Lodestone.

Why do you carry a drawing of it, Calene?"

"It's just a rock to me—one with a great big tree growing out of it—and that's all. You said you knew what it was though, so why don't you tell me about it, *Brina*?"

"Brina," the Banished repeated, pointing at the elf.

"There's a reason so few of us have the Spark," Brina started, eyeing the Banished and giving him a small, shy smile. "It's dying, even without the Empire murdering elven children with potential. War doesn't agree with us, and neither does living as slaves or in slums. Our magic is failing, and it drives those that possess it to fight harder. Our elders speak of another kind of magic, something that doesn't live on the inside like the Spark. They say, millennia ago, we...communicated with the nature around us. No, wait. Communication isn't the right word. Why is your language so limited? Look, we're a part of it, and we wielded it as an extension of ourselves, but it also wielded us."

"You were wielded by nature?"

"I don't know if that's the right word, but... We didn't worship magic as some separate being, like your Sparker Order do with Raas and Janna. We acted as one. Together."

"Talk straight, elf," Calene snapped. "The Spark *does* involve nature. I feel it when I reach out with my senses, everywhere I go."

"Listen, you borrow, yes? And if you take too much, you can damage yourselves. A Sparker can only hold so much, like a boat. Fill it with too much water and the hulls will crack, or it becomes too heavy and sinks."

"Something like that," Calene muttered, eyeing the wood walls and wishing she'd picked a different analogy.

"The Elders told us of the songs the ancients would use, a way of communicating, harnessing nature itself. As long as we lived in balance, acted in peace and didn't use it for violence, nature provided for us. We could grow trees with the song, fill fields with grain, build our homes. Until the first wars, with those you call the Banished. When we called upon our magic to aid us, it resisted and faltered. Our mages learned how to harness the Spark within them, but we lost our balance with nature. The old songs, the old magic, disappeared and now the Spark is dying, too. So the Elders say."

"Singing," Calene said, tapping a finger against her lip and staring at the Banished. "Huh. Alright, maybe, in these olden days, according to your Elders, if you wanted to heal someone, you'd ask nature to do that too? And if you did it real polite-like, it would agree."

Brina followed Calene's gaze to the man from beyond Solitude and frowned. "Yes."

"Interesting." Calene took the sheet of paper from her pocket and stared at her etching. "So what's the Lode-stone?"

"The source, Calene," Brina said. "The spring from which our magic, even nature itself, flowed. Stories spoke of it, though we thought it lost. Not many elves believe in it at all now."

"Calene," the Banished said, pointing at her. He looked at the sleeping Sparker on the bed. "Vettigan."

"Yes, yes, well done.," Calene grunted. "Look, I have an idea where your Lodestone is. An old Sparker drew this rock and tree. He claimed he found it in the Peaks of Eternity. Watch."

She held the drawing up for the Banished to see.

"Muir!" he cried, wonder in his face. "Muir! Muir!"

"I think he recognises it," Brina said.

"Where?" Calene asked, tapping the drawing and holding it closer to the Banished. "Where is Muir?"

The man grabbed his sword and pointed at the emblem on the crossguard, his fingernail tapping at the engraving.

"Solitude," he whispered.

Calene folded the paper.

"Calene," she said, pointing to herself, then at the others in the cabin. "Brina. Vettigan."

Then she thrust a finger at him.

"Tilo," he replied, a broad grin on his face.

"Brina," Calene said, not taking her eyes from Tilo's, "try to talk to him. Find words you both understand. It's important we figure him out."

"Yes," Brina agreed. "Can I have the picture?"

Calene gave it over, and the elf took it, hands trembling.

"I never believed," she whispered. "Or maybe I did, and lost my faith."

"God's teeth, what's all this racket, and where the drok are we? The Underworld? Are we on a boat? Are we all dead or did you just decide to join me for the ride?"

Calene's heart leapt into her mouth. She turned to see Vettigan, propped on one elbow, scowling at them.

"Vettigan, thank the gods you're all right." She jumped to her feet and banged her head on the ceiling of their cabin. Rubbing her aching crown, she rushed to his side. "We're heading to Solitude."

Vettigan leaned over and spat on the floor, right between her boots.

"Damn the gods," he growled, eyes blazing. He glared at her a moment longer, then rolled to face the wall. "You should have left me to die."

Calene reached out to him, but stopped, tears welling in her eyes. Embracing her Second Sight, she saw the shadow Tilo had reduced still lingered on the Sparker's brain. It pulsated now that he'd awoken, battling against the barrier encircling it.

It's twisting his thoughts. Twisting him. *Gods have mercy.*

"Give him time," Brina whispered, lacing her fingers with Calene's and squeezing them.

"Drok off and let me sleep," Vettigan grunted.

Tears dripped from Calene's chin as she got to her feet and left the cabin, arms wrapped around her stomach. Standing on the deck, she leaned against the rail and closed her eyes. Brine sprayed her face, a weight in her stomach, as she let herself weep.

The sun sat high in the sky, but the wind took away its heat. Calene tried to lose herself in the ship's gentle rocking as it cut its way through the water, attempting to empty her mind of thoughts, but she couldn't. She wanted to believe Brina, that Vettigan needed time. But she saw the shadow inside him, saw the hatred in his eyes.

Calene reached towards the part of her mind connected with Vettigan, a tentative caress. A storm of curses and filth rushed back through their Link and she recoiled. She threw up a hasty barrier and tried not to be sick. His thoughts had never been like that before. So dark, so angry, so faithless and hopeless and violent. It felt like she'd poked a hole through something rotten and the stain of it lingered on her. Shadows smothered her friend's mind, devouring the light and the comfort she'd always found in him.

She leaned against the bulwark and choked out a sob.

Vettigan may live, she thought, *but the man I knew is dead.*

CHAPTER TEN
COLD TURKEY

'I'd rather throw myself overboard and plummet into the icy depths, than give up the spice. And that's the truth.' - The words of a drowned, Octarian spice-addicted sailor.

Kade lay on his bunk, tossing and turning in sweat-slick sheets. The stifling heat inside the cabin and the pain from his broken ankle didn't help his fever, nor did the bottles of Avastian brandy he'd guzzled. Kade burned, but the chill inside his bones made him shiver. His stomach twisted and cramped and the alcohol came back in acidic eruptions. He felt as though, if he reached out, he could clasp Rune's slender hand.

His mind flickered to the spice box falling to the street, kicked out of his reach.

Now the spice made him pay for his clumsiness, the decision he'd made to abandon it.

At first, the pain from his ankle had distracted him. Then came the hatchet job of repair courtesy of the ship's cook, a muscular brute of a man—from Octaria, of all places— which only made the agony worse.

The cook strapped Kade's forehead and limbs to the bed. Placing his tobacco stick between his lips, he'd grunted two words.

"Brace yourself."

The cook twisted Kade's ankle like he'd wrench the head from a doll and Kade screamed, veins popping in his neck and forehead as his vision blurred and dimmed. He'd wanted to vomit. He heard—felt—the crack of bones crunching back into place. His 'doctor' held the ankle in place as he strapped it to a makeshift splint, then left Kade with three bottles of brandy.

"Keep your weight off it and drink. The pain will keep you awake otherwise."

Since then—two days ago, Kade thought—the ship's crew had left him alone, save for a cabin boy who brought him fresh water and food. Most of that went untouched. In his more lucid moments, Kade forced chunks of cheese and bread into his dry mouth, but his rebelling stomach soon forced it back up.

His ankle and knees throbbed as he reached for the brandy. Grabbing an empty one, Kade flung it against the cabin door and laughed as it shattered to pieces. He fumbled for another, fingers landing on a half-full bottle. The sweet liquid trickled down his throat and spilled over his lips, mixing with the thickening stubble on his chin.

Kade's eyes drooped, and the bottle fell from his hand with a clatter as he slid into an uneasy sleep.

"Why did you send me away, father?"

Kade creaked his crusted eyes open. Arlo sat across his stomach, like he'd done as a toddler, staring into his face. He held a dagger to Kade's throat.

"Son, how—"

"Were you ashamed of me? Scared your friends would find out about my elven whore mother? Did my dirty blood sicken you?"

"No," Kade whispered. His son's eyes were black with hatred. A part of his brain noticed the cabin didn't rock and sway as it had earlier, though he heard the wind howl outside and the stench of rotting meat assailed his nostrils.

"A problem sent away, that's what I am. One meaningless mistake soon rectified by the swing of a Banished's mace."

Arlo turned his head to the side. His skull gaped open where the flesh had ripped away, exposing crushed bone and mashed brain. Blood matted his dirty-blonde hair and stained his neck and cloak crimson.

Kade raised a trembling hand to touch his son, but Arlo snarled and plunged the dagger into his windpipe.

He surged upwards as intense pain erupted in his throat. Choking, he gripped his neck, desperate to hold the blood inside. Kade looked around. Arlo had vanished. The pain faded and he stared at his bloodless fingers in disbelief. No wound, no blade. The stench of rot prevailed.

"Did you love me, Kade?" a melodic voice asked. One he knew well and had longed to hear again. The voice dripped with scorn and disgust. "Or did you just convince yourself you did to ease your guilty conscience after droking a filthy elf?"

Kade rubbed his forehead, peering through his fingers. Arlo's mother stood in the open cabin doorway. She wore a simple, white shift; the colour standing out against her tanned skin and bright red hair. Rune stood as beautiful and elegant as he remembered and he longed for her, but the sneer on her lips turned him cold.

"All those gifts. The dresses and flowers. You kept me like a pet. Did using me make you feel more like a man? No expectations with an elf. No chance of being tied down with responsibility to another family. You could have your fun and discard me any time you wanted."

"Rune, it wasn't like that," Kade moaned, falling from the bed and crawling to her on hands and knees. He wondered why the glass hadn't cut her bare feet, but when he looked, he couldn't see the shards of the broken bottle on the floor. "I loved you. More than anything. I didn't want to keep you. I wanted to *free* you. I'd have traded everything for you."

"So you said." Rune stepped forward and took Kade's head in her hands. He never thought she'd touch him again. Despite it all, he leaned into her grasp. "But you didn't free me, did you? You kept me until the bitter end. I died a slave, in a cage, and you held the key."

"The time wasn't right." He whispered the words

without conviction, staring into her green eyes. "It wasn't safe."

"Excuses. So many excuses. You're craven, Kade. You always were. And now, because of your cowardice, I am dead and my son will soon join me. We could have been safe, with our own kind, or in Avastia. If we could only have escaped from you."

She pressed her hands against his skull and pain blossomed in his head. He felt his cranium splitting and aching from the pressure.

"I'm sorry," Kade gasped, vision turning red. He refused to struggle. Her words rang true; he deserved his fate.

"You sent away your only reminder of me. Did it hurt too much to look at our son?"

"Yes," Kade breathed, eyeballs bulging.

Just as he thought they'd pop, he fell forward onto his face, crashing against the wooden floor. He staggered up on all fours and shook his head, bile oozing from his mouth. The cabin door stood open. A blast of icy wind blew through.

"You had to involve me, didn't you, boy?"

A rasping, wet voice. A familiar voice. Kade turned to his bunk. The stench of rot made him gag, but he couldn't pull his eyes from the sight in front of him even as they filled with tears.

Bertrand lay there, a hideous ruin, stomach torn, intestines exposed and draped over his torso. Blood dripped from the mess of his body onto the floor. The old man's lifeless eyes stared at Kade; his mouth hung open exposing a chasm of broken teeth and mutilated tongue. His voice echoed around the cabin.

"We had to fight," Kade said, pushing himself to his feet. He waited for his ankle to buckle but it held strong.

"Like you battled against Nexes in the Conclave meeting?" Bertrand bellowed, dead eyes accusing. "You rolled over and showed him your yellow belly."

"My son. He knew—"

"Excuses!" The dead man's hand flopped towards Kade, a stiff, blackened finger pointing at him. "Did you ever care about anything other than protecting yourself? Do you go north to hide in the Gallavan Forests and hope life forgets you?"

"No," Kade growled, "I go for my son. I should never have sent him away."

"Correct," Bertrand said, heaving himself to his feet.

The smell of decaying flesh washed over Kade and his throat tightened, guts rippling, as the corpse shuffled towards him. Its entrails spilled out and swung between its knees. Bertrand slipped on the blood-slick floor, but kept coming. Kade backed away, but his gaze remained fixed on the horror moving toward him.

"You're a weakling. A hypocrite. You hated that we warred with the elves, yet your family kept slaves. Droked them, too. You think Rune loved you? No, she let you lust over her for a chance at survival. You despise war, but turn a blind eye even with Haltveldt decimating every duchy on this continent, and your precious Octaria in their sights.

Avastia, too. They'll ruin the world, and you're happy to watch so long as you're not under scrutiny. So long as no one knows your precious secrets."

Kade reached for the cabin door. It slammed closed behind him. Panic surged and he seized the handle, wrestling with it in the desperate hope it would open. But it didn't and he faced the nightmare. Bertrand inched forward.

"And what are you going to do when you reach Solitude?" the corpse hissed. "What can one man do? Hasn't that always been your mantra, *Master* Kade? What can one man do against centuries of hate for the elven people? What can one man do against the mob at the gates to the Elven Quarter? What can one man do against an Empire? Why would you stand up and fight now, of all times? If you'd loved your boy, you wouldn't have sent him away in the first place. He's going to die. And you're going to die with him."

Kade fell backwards through the doorway. Wind howled and rain battered from the black sky, so forceful it threatened to beat him into the deck. But he didn't stand on a ship. His hands felt frigid, wet rock beneath them. Kade blinked. Although he'd never journeyed there before, he knew with utter conviction he stood upon Solitude's walls.

He gazed around. From his vantage upon Solitude's highest point, at the centre of its walls, Kade saw the Peaks of Eternity towering in the distance, like splayed fingers attached to an enormous hand reaching up into the sky, curling around to squeeze the fortress at either side. Before them, an ocean of Banished, stretching back to the distant mountains. The horde screamed as one with the wind, terrible weapons raised above their heads.

"How are we meant to stand against so many?" Kade whispered. He stood at the wall's edge, a voice in the back of his head urging him to jump as he stared at the throng below.

"Father."

Kade spun. Arlo stood across the rampart. An elf, tall and strong, an eerie echo of Rune's blazing hair and piercing eyes and graceful beauty, draped an arm around his shoulder, but Kade knew it wasn't her because this woman didn't feel the same. A tall, pale man with yellow eyes held his son's hand.

"Son," Kade said, taking a step forward.

"Don't worry," the pale warrior said. "You'll understand his purpose."

The tall man leapt from the wall, pulling Arlo and the elf with him. Kade yelled and ran to where they'd fallen. He stared into the forest beyond but only two sets of footprints in the sparse snow led into the thin woods beyond. Of the elf, he saw no sign.

"Thought I'd find you here," Nexes called.

Kade drew his sword and turned to face the Master of War. "Raas damn you."

"You want this?" the man asked, holding a small snuff box between a thumb and finger. "You left it behind."

Nexes placed it on the wall overlooking the Banished

hordes. Kade took a step, a lurch as the drug called to him. He staggered again and dropped his sword, falling forward and reaching out for his spice. Kade slammed into the low wall and cradled the box, lifting it to his nose as his hands trembled.

A piercing pain bit into his spine and tore through his chest. He looked down to see bloody steel erupting between his ribs.

"Elf-lover," Nexes whispered in his ear. He wrenched his sword clear of Kade's body and tipped him over the wall.

Kade fell. For hours, spinning into a sea of faces howling and screaming and cursing him. He crashed into water and gasped as his mouth and nostrils filled with liquid. Kade screamed as he drowned in an ocean of Banished.

�— ◆ —⌐

"Sir, calm down." Kade wrenched his eyes open and found himself staring at the cabin boy. Water dripped from his hair down his forehead, and he shivered. "You were screaming and wouldn't wake when I shook you. Had to throw a bucket on you."

Kade fell back onto his soaking bed. A choking laugh erupted from his throat. It grew louder, and he howled and cried. The cabin boy backed away as Kade curled into a ball, his ankle protesting at the movement, as his tears mingled with the water on his face.

⟨⚬────────◆────────⚬⟩

Nightmares plagued him, vivid visions from his past. Arlo, Rune, Bertrand, and so many other regrets. Too many to count. Too many to name. None of it felt as real as that first night.

On the morning of their fourth day at sea, Kade heard the cries of the sailors as the ship approached Adhraas docks, the nearest harbour to Solitude. The shouts woke him; he felt tired but free of the more severe withdrawal symptoms. The dreams had settled to meaningless nonsense and his stomach cramps had eased. His hands trembled less than before, and a pressure thumped behind his left temple, but he thought the worst to be over.

Adhraas lay some ten miles to Solitude's south, and Kade hadn't thought about how he'd reach it yet. He hobbled to retrieve his cloak and fasten it across his shoulders. He grimaced when he placed even the lightest of pressure on his ankle. Ten miles might as well have been a thousand. He pictured Arlo, head caved in like it had been in the dream.

I'll crawl if I must.

He left his cabin and made his way to the deck, watching as the crew brought the ship in. Seagulls cried in the icy air, and he tasted salt. Blue skies stretched for miles above, and his breath fogged from his lips. Kade rubbed his hands and waited to disembark. The captain, another Octarian, extended the gangplank, then stood speaking with a waiting messenger. He glanced Kade's way and waved with a gentle smile.

"A word, my friend," he said, laying an arm across Kade's shoulders and steering him to the ship's bulwark facing the harbour. "Away from the crew. There's word from the south you need to hear."

He peered around as Kade watched another ship cut through the harbour, bringing more people into Adhraas.

"Why do I feel like this won't be good?" Kade asked, managing a smile at the captain. The Octarian stared back with dull eyes.

"Sorry, my friend," he said, squeezing Kade's shoulder. "You shouldn't have made an enemy of Master Nexes. His reach is long."

The captain jammed something into Kade's stomach. The air escaped his lungs in a rush. He tried to cough but tasted warm iron in his mouth. Saliva wet his chin. He touched it with a gloved hand and stared at it.

Red, he thought, confused. *But...*

The captain thrust again, multiple times, quick movements. Kade slumped against the rail, wrestling for the blade with blood-slick hands. His brain caught up.

He's murdering me.

Kade reached for the sword at his hip. Rough hands grabbed him from behind and tossed him over the rail. He plunged headfirst into the harbour, and darkness devoured him.

CHAPTER ELEVEN
THE CRIMES OF WAR

'In war, there's nothing more sacred than talking under the white flag of truce. Until Spring Haven became an Empire. Then it all changed.' - From the banned texts of Eren, a historian from the old Hiberian Duchy, now part of the Haltveldt Empire.

"Garet says they're not attacking at full force yet," Arlo said, his breath visible in the crisp morning air.

"For once," Zanna replied, "I agree with him."

Her apprentice had brought food and water after her nightshift on the ramparts. The Sparkers toiled day and night to ensure their magical shield remained strong. Garet tasked others with mixing fire into the shield, designed to disintegrate arrows and other projectiles that the Banished fired. Great gusts of wind tunnelled in front of the walls, keeping their attackers away.

Zanna appreciated the modifications to the shield; the original, erected in haste, would only block magic and dampen sound. Now, they had more protection, though it came at a cost. Every Sparker poured their focus into maintaining it, day and night. No one knew how the shield would cope under a sustained assault.

Not that the Banished appeared keen to take the initiative. Zanna watched them through her telescope, studying the swathes of fighters to the rear of their ranks, standing between the non-combatants and the Peaks. They'd spent the first day manoeuvring their people into that curious position and she still couldn't guess why.

She had to credit Garet. His plans were shrewd. He'd led several Sparkers to collapse huge trenches of earth along Solitude's walls to keep the Banished from storming the fortress. They would need siege weapons now and the building would delay their offensive perhaps for weeks.

If there even is *an offensive.*

Garet had split the two hundred Sparkers into squads of five and stationed them along the walls within line of sight. Reserve teams waited below to relieve their friends when needed. Zanna's relief would come soon, but she appreciated the food from her apprentice. Arlo had taken to the task of message runner.

"I've said it before, but the Banished sure like waiting, master," Arlo said, cupping a steaming mug of hot chocolate.

"They don't want to waste lives," Zanna replied. "You're here in the heavens, staring down. Imagine their point of view; gazing up at towering walls filled with an army of sorcerers."

"But we don't have an army."

"They don't know that. They're prudent, and like you said, they're waiting for something," Zanna said, biting into a chunk of bread. "Right now, that looks like nightfall. It follows the pattern."

The limited skirmishes had taken place at night, under cover of darkness. The Banished, apart from sending warriors to their rear, built their arsenal to break a siege—trebuchets, catapults, ladders. Once they'd realised what the Sparkers had done, they'd focused a volley of projectiles on specific parts of the shield wall, testing for weaknesses. No blood had spilled, but the Sparkers grew tired from the constant concentration. They knew the Banished would exploit even the smallest crack in their defence.

Zanna gazed through the haze of dancing fire at the Banished. Estimates marked their number at five hundred thousand, though a third of that appeared to be non-combatants—children, elders and those with child.

I was right, she thought. *This is a migration. They want out of their prison. But their leaders value their lives; their reticence to attack proves that much. Many armies would throw their soldiers at the walls.*

Haltveldt would throw its soldiers at the walls. Men, women, children—whoever they could so long as they snatched victory.

"I dreamt about them again last night," Arlo murmured.

Zanna's attention snapped to her apprentice. The nights had been long of late; inky shadows circled his pinched, pasty skin. The boy stared toward the Banished, but his dull eyes gazed through them.

"The singing?" Zanna asked. She felt a flicker in her section's defences, a slight weakening. She focused her energy into the shield wall.

"Yes," he replied, in a monotone. "The lights up there too. They...tore again. Split across the sky, but the colours faded. A bright, white column rose up, touching the heavens, but behind it darkness waited. And...the picture we found, the rock with the tree. It calls to me."

Zanna gazed towards the horizon. Even in daylight and through the haze of shimmering, magical fire, she saw the heavens above the Peaks of Eternity writhing with a multitude of colours, a bruise on the sky high above the range. The Banished watched it too. Garet insisted they had caused the maelstrom, a signal of sorts. Zanna didn't think so. When she watched them through her telescope, she recognised their fear.

"I'm not so sure these are dreams anymore, Arlo," she said, laying a hand on her apprentice's shoulder. "You're having the same dreams every night, and so vividly?"

"I hear them singing right now," he whispered, drawing his cloak closer around his thin body. "Or it."

Drok, Zanna thought. *There's something I've missed here.*

She considered his words, his behaviour since the Banished had appeared, even his advancing Spark, which made unmatched strides every day. Arlo had appeared shocked and frightened that first night, but the experience had lit a fire in him. He'd thrown himself into his research, which hadn't surprised her as his love of books and study had shone through from the moment Zanna met him.

Then he'd discovered Matrim the Mad's journals and the dreams he'd mentioned since arriving at Solitude had only grown more intense. Arlo had withdrawn into himself even as his Spark bloomed.

"Perhaps you should leave with the servants when they depart for Adhraas? You can help start the evacuation."

"No," Arlo shouted, his body trembling as soon as the suggestion left Zanna's lips. "I can't. Don't make me, Zanna."

The conviction startled her. The boy bunched his hands into fists by his side, pupils drowning out the blue of his eyes.

Teeth of the gods. How have I let it come to this? I told myself to spend more time with him. I've been so worried about Calene and the Banished and the vote, I hadn't even realised what was happening to him.

"Sorry, Arlo," she whispered, stooping and laying a hand on his cheek. Her black skin stood out against his too-pale face. "I've failed you. You'll stay at Solitude, with me."

Arlo relaxed and sagged against her. The sudden change made ice run through her veins.

"Thank you, master."

"Go and rest," she said, "now. That's an order."

Arlo nodded. Zanna watched him slink away, slumped and head down.

Raas, and any other of you motherless gods listening, she prayed, turning back to the Banished, *don't dare let any harm befall that boy. Don't let him pay for my mistakes.*

———◆———

Zanna tossed and turned, drifting in and out of sleep. She'd trained her mind to focus its energies on the wall, even in slumber, but that wasn't what made her rest fitful.

Arlo's state of mind worried her. Sparkers often experienced vivid dreams, and the Order's histories mentioned some who'd suffered from premonitions and foresight in the past. A lost gift, though the chronicles had described it more like a burden. She considered the possibility that Arlo's dreams were actually latent prophetic powers, but it could equally have been the proximity of the Banished and the Peaks of Eternity. He trembled at the mere thought of being sent away from Solitude.

There's a link there, Zanna thought, staring up at the ceiling. *I wish I'd realised sooner.*

As ever, it wasn't just Arlo on her mind. Calene dominated her thoughts. She couldn't establish the Link with her without breaking her concentration on the shield wall. It pained her, but she couldn't allow her focus to slip, even for a moment. For all Zanna knew, the Banished Calene had found had turned on her, but she put her abrupt departure in their last Link down to Zanna overstepping her boundaries too often. She didn't want to consider the alternative.

She hoped they'd reach Spring Haven and convince the Conclave to act.

I can't help but think of her, she mused, twisting the blankets between her fingers in frustration. *I'd given up hope of reconnecting with her. Now I have, but under circumstances such as these... Calene, will I ever see you again?*

Zanna sighed. Lying in bed wouldn't solve the conundrum of the Banished. It wouldn't help Arlo's situation, and she grew weary of pining over her daughter.

I can do more, she thought, flinging the fur covers aside.

Zanna removed her white shift, bare feet padding on the stone floor, and washed, before dressing in her favourite purple robes. The words she'd spoken to Garet returned to her, over and again, goading her.

"Have you tried talking to them?"

To Zanna, it seemed so simple. A way to avoid bloodshed before the inevitable happened. The Banished seemed intent on breaching Solitude and heading south. If she could discover why then perhaps no one would need to die. She inspected her reflection in the mirror. She could live for another two hundred years, at least.

Could. Nothing's ever certain.

She nodded to herself, breathed deep and left.

———◇———

"Zanna, you're not on duty," Garet grunted, pulling her aside by the elbow as she ascended the steps to Solitude's tallest rampart. She'd decided to approach her superior one last time, before she took matters into her own hands. "What brings you here?"

She gazed downwards at the Banished front lines, three hundred paces from Solitude's walls. The trench gaped between them, an unbridgeable rift.

"I want to know why you won't seek peace with them."

She expected anger and defiance. Instead, Garet shook his head and pursed his lips.

"This isn't a peaceful world," he said, letting his stare wander across the Sparkers maintaining the shield wall. "We've often found ourselves at odds. Perhaps my exile, a century ago, reminds you too much of your own actions? Whatever you think of me, consider this. Solitude is my home."

"It's mine too," Zanna said.

"For a decade. I've lived here a hundred years. These Sparkers are my people." He pointed south, toward Adhraas. "You, that apprentice of yours and the simple folk who live beyond these walls are my responsibility. I'm the Protector of Solitude. That's my title. My duty. And it remains my duty, no matter how the Conclave tie my hands more and more with each passing year. Now, they've finally granted us a boon. We can use our full potential, for the first time without fear of recrimination from the Council. I must deal with the facts as I see them. A nation of Banished are here, and they've made it clear they seek to pass, one way or another. I only want to protect my people, Zanna. Can't you see that? I realise you may think me rash, arrogant, but I do what I see is right. For the greater good."

"Then find another way," she replied, clasping her hands. "Talk to them."

"Do they look like they want to talk?" Garet snapped. He tossed his head towards the Banished. "Don't the swords and spears and siege weapons spell it out for you? Don't the unprovoked attacks make it plain? They're invaders, and we must treat them as such."

She smiled at Garet. *I pity you,* she thought, staring into eyes that always held only anger. *Calene, Arlo. I do this for you.*

Zanna turned on her heel, wind whipping around her as she strode across Solitude's highest rampart. Her cloak billowed, grey-streaked hair streaming behind her. The other Sparkers on duty turned her way, surprise on their faces. Without pausing, she opened herself to the energies flowing around the fortress—life, fear, water, air and earth. The dying embers of hope. She let it build inside her until she trembled with the excess of power, more alive, more connected than ever before. Drawing it all in, she felt the limits of what she could hold straining. Only her daughter could exceed those boundaries. Energies of all kinds swirled around Solitude, and she felt it all, used it all. She'd need it.

Climbing atop the rampart, Zanna stepped off.

She wove her magic as she did, ignoring the gasps and cries of alarm from the Sparkers on the walls, and drove the maelstrom of energy building inside her outwards.

Wind to support her, to push her through the shield

wall. A barrier to protect her, like the one she'd created for Arlo's experiments, from the conflagration swirling between Solitude and the Banished. She saw the warriors a hundred feet below pointing up in wonder as she glided through the air, heard the yells of her fellow Sparkers as she descended, but she ignored them.

She scanned the ground, senses magnified as the Spark powered her, looking for the Banished leader who'd waited closest to the walls. She saw him, features standing out in exquisite detail—the pulse vibrating in his neck, the flecks of white in his yellow-fair hair, the worry lines eating into his noble face. He gazed back. As she drifted closer, she saw his wide, grey eyes fill with tears of astonishment.

She understood. A mage appearing from the sky, alone, to face down an entire army. There had to be apprehension. But she noticed something else in his stare too. She felt it in the air.

Hope.

Zanna's bare feet met the ground, for the first time in a decade. The sensation thrilled her, and she almost forgot herself as she wriggled her toes in the grass.

I've deprived myself of simple pleasures for too long, she thought, watching the Banished leader, *all because I've punished myself for protecting my daughter. I should have found another way, yes. But I'm wiser, and I'll show everyone I'm no monster.*

She'd landed in the midst of an army. The thought struck her with its full consequence when she looked around at the hundreds of pale faces all around, and the thousands more beyond them. Still holding onto her Spark, she felt the energy build from the army. Fear, yes. Determination. Hope. It all called to her.

As did something else. A distant curiosity. Watching. Waiting...

It vanished, as if it knew it had been noticed. Zanna shook the distraction off and focused on the Banished.

"How dare you?" Garet screamed from up high on the walls. His amplified voice carried over the wind. "You fool!"

Zanna ignored him.

The Banished leader stepped forward to meet her. Others tried to follow but he waved them back. He pointed at Zanna and uttered a few words in his language that she couldn't understand. He approached and stopped just beyond arm's reach.

She studied him. He had a strength about him—not just physical, though he stood tall and appeared muscled beneath his armour. No, his power went deeper than that somehow. He appeared to have hit middle age, though she realised his ivory skin and near-colourless hair rendered him almost ageless. His eyes held the weight of wisdom, just as his features held the lines of age.

She glanced at the sword he wore at his hip. The weapon glinted in the daylight, and she noticed a relief of Solitude engraved on its crossguard.

Zanna turned and looked behind her, craning her neck to stare up at the towering walls, the tallest rampart one hundred feet above. She saw Sparkers leaning over, the glass of their telescopes reflecting the sunlight.

An unnatural hush descended on the plains. Zanna could hear the rustle of chain mail and the whinny of horses, though cries from Solitude drifted to her from above.

"I've never seen it from this side," she said, smiling at the Banished before studying the fortress.

It towered above them, a stone monstrosity with impassable, barred gates large enough to accommodate ten soldiers side-by-side, and the new trench like a chasm into the bowels of the earth. Intimidating enough, but the Peaks of Eternity dwarfed even them, sweeping behind the Banished, until they built to their highest point in the far distance. The mass of swirling colours still hovered above them. An ominous, unwelcoming view.

She felt so small, so insignificant, staring up at the sheer fortress walls, the craggy mountains, but still she felt liberated. For the first time in a decade, Zanna had acted instead of hiding. An exile she might have been, but a Sparker too, and a servant of the gods.

She laid a hand against her chest. "Zanna."

The Banished nodded and mimicked her gesture. "Kearn," he replied, voice deep and musical.

Zanna stared at him, then let her gaze drift to the people assembled behind him. She pointed at them.

"Why?"

Kearn turned and pointed to the summit of the Peaks of Eternity, and the maelstrom coalescing there. Zanna forced her eyes upwards and a moment of panic gripped her.

Our fortress on one side, and those terrible mountains on the other, she thought, breathing to steady herself. *Oppression no matter where they look.*

"Il Renuish," Kearn said, facing her again. He crossed his wrists together, forming an X, then moved his palms in a straight line. "Solitude harran va liesh."

"Il Renuish?" Zanna asked, trying to duplicate his accent. She couldn't tell if she succeeded or not.

"Vah," Kearn replied, nodding and smiling. He pointed to the top of Solitude. Zanna turned. She saw Garet standing there, robes and raven hair billowing in the wind. "Tilo? Bur pashea il Muir."

"I'm sorry," Zanna said, shaking her head with a wry smile, "I've no idea what you're saying."

Kearn laughed, a beautiful sound that made her heart soar. He pointed at her, then at himself, and raised a hand to his mouth.

"Ret?"

"Eat," Zanna said, and smiled. "Yes, please."

Kearn turned and called to the Banished behind him. Several of them broke ranks.

This is working, Zanna thought, hope blooming in her chest. *There is more to this. They don't want to fight!*

The Banished glanced back to her and the smile on his face disintegrated, eyes growing wide.

"Sha!" he yelled, shoving Zanna backwards. As she crashed into the mud, she saw Garet, felt his magic as he stood upon the walls, arms raised in triumph.

A fireball struck the ground where she'd been standing and erupted, searing shrapnel flying in all directions. Zanna scrambled away on all fours. Kearn lay dazed in the dirt. The projectile had hit the ground under him and tossed him into the air. At least, it had tossed his torso into the air. His legs were just...gone. His hands moved feebly for a moment, head twisting, trying to check on his people.

She crawled to him and cradled his head. More dead, dying, burning bodies lay strewn in the mud behind him, and the cries of those still living ate into her soul. Embers danced in the air around them and a mist of blood and ash fogged the killing field.

Those people were bringing me food. Food! Why, Garet? Why?

Kearn gasped as she gazed into his eyes.

"Il Renuish," he breathed, reaching for her face. He grazed her cheeks. "Solitude...death."

His hand dropped as the light fled from his eyes.

"Death..." Zanna repeated, tears stinging her eyes as sound exploded around her.

The Banished, two hundred yards away, rattled their weapons and wailed. Maces, swords and spears glinted in the sunlight, and they cried as one for the death of those who sought peace, murdered by the Sparkers of Solitude.

She felt it before she heard it. The air seemed to hold its breath around her as a hundred Sparkers drew from the world all at once. Then, it erupted.

Fire poured from the walls as they let loose, raining flame upon the Banished's front ranks. The heat scorched Zanna's skin and stung her eyes.

Garet had won. They'd attacked.

She heard the screams of burning soldiers. Death on a scale she had never seen, even on the elvish front. Horns sounded in the distance and invisible hands grasped her, dragged her from the ground. She let go of Kearn's head as she floated up towards Solitude's walls.

Tears flooded down her cheeks as she watched the conflagration devour the Banished as they attempted to flee.

If I'd stayed on the walls... she thought. *I gave Garet a reason to attack. I tried to do the right thing, Raas believe me. I thought there was a better way.*

Her feet touched stone, already forgetting the sensation of earth and grass beneath them, and she sank to the floor of Solitude's highest rampart. She covered her eyes but couldn't shut out the noises of the destruction. The roar of the flames; the keening of the dying.

Garet stood above her, arms stretched wide. His coterie surrounded him as they conducted a symphony of death in the plains below. Glee, fury and madness danced across his features.

"Drok the vote," he snarled. "This is war. How dare they attack a lone Sparker who approached in peace? They'll pay. Raas smiles on me!"

"We were talking," Zanna choked, Kearn's fading smile seared into her soul. "He sent for food."

"I know what I saw," Garet replied, gazing at the chaos below like a fond father watching their child play. "They planned to kill you. I won't let a Sparker die like some elf in a ditch. Now they'll tremble at our might."

She crawled to the ledge and pulled herself up. Smoke rose from the charred bodies beyond Kearn's corpse. The Banished had fled to a safe distance and were trying to regroup. Zanna tasted death on the air.

More would follow. Garet had the excuse he needed now, all thanks to her.

War fed more war. Evil nourished evil. She knew it, felt it in her soul the night she'd Eviscerated Ricken. She sensed the energies of the other Sparkers washing over her as they committed genocide—hatred, aggression, glee.

It could only end in one way. Disaster.

Calene, I tried, Zanna thought. *Please, believe me. I tried.*

⸎

Zanna stayed on the wall for hours, not speaking, just watching.

Garet called off the attack once it became clear the Banished wouldn't launch a counter. The Sparkers continued their vigil. Arlo joined her at one point, but errands called him away. Neither of them spoke.

As the sun set, the Banished sang. Their voices joined and washed over Solitude. An unnatural darkness smothered the sky and the only light came from the ever-present swirl of colour above the mountains.

Zanna heard rumbling in the distance and peered through her telescope. Illuminated by the lights in the heavens, more Banished poured over the foothills, bringing with them enormous ranged weapons and siege ladders, long enough to reach the tops of Solitude's ramparts, and wagons carrying rocks and wood to pour into the trench.

They'd prepared for battle, even if they hadn't sought it.

Word spread between Solitude's defenders before the first catapult, a thousand feet away, launched its projectile into the Sparkers' shield. The barrier pulsed as the boulder disintegrated, though flecks of shale rained through.

More followed, arcing through the sky, slamming into the shield with mighty booms. Zanna opened her Second Sight and scanned the ramparts. Beacons of magic—the Sparkers—shone bright in the darkness. She saw their wall pulsate as the projectiles hit, quivering but standing strong. Then the attacks stopped. So did the singing.

When she'd met Kearn, she'd peered into his misty eyes and seen peace in his spirit, but she'd also recognised his other qualities. The leader, yes, and the spokesman, but also the warrior. His people were of one mind. They didn't want a drawn-out siege.

Their catapults fired once more, targeting a strip of the wall to Zanna's right, focusing their efforts on one area. They'd learned from their prodding of the invisible barrier. The projectiles hit together and tore through, punching into Solitude's ramparts. Boulders as large as the Sparkers themselves crashed to the earth below, tumbling into the trench or tearing ragged gaps in the fortress.

Zanna saw beacons flicker and die as the projectiles

killed Sparkers where they hit. The shield wall flickered, as the remaining poured their magic into it, straining to keep it strong and whole. More projectiles followed as the Banished's war cries ripped through the black afternoon.

"We won't last a day," Zanna whispered, throwing every ounce of Spark she had into the wall, "and it's all my fault."

CHAPTER TWELVE
PURPOSE

'As one, we follow in his steps.' - The motto of the Followers of
Raas, a sect with strong ties to the Sparker Order, though the
Council downplays those links of late.

C alene stood on the deck as her ship approached
Adhraas harbour. Another vessel had dropped anchor, and she scanned the bustle around the docks and the
town beyond with narrow eyes.

Would have thought they'd have evacuated by now, she
thought. *The Sparkers and the army at Solitude should keep
them safe, but waiting around is madness. It's like nothing's
changed here.*

The giant statue of Raas dominated Adhraas, standing
tall and proud, arms spread to encompass the town that
bore his name. The holy books claimed it as the god's place
of birth, aeons before, and the locals took great pride in it.
Sparkers, the ones that believed, would make pilgrimage
there early in their training with the Order, little knowing
they'd end up stationed in that fortress on the horizon one

day, if they lived long enough or droked up too badly.

Looming in the distance were the Peaks of Eternity. Strange lights tinted the clouds above them and staring at them gave her an ache in her back teeth. Dead weight settled in her guts.

Calene prodded the Link with her mother again. They were so close now. It felt like a comforting weight in her pocket, a keepsake of their bond, though Zanna still didn't respond. That gave her a different feeling she couldn't shake. A sense that something had gone wrong. Calene tried to dismiss it, telling herself the Emperor's army had arrived already and bolstered the ranks, but the nagging thought wouldn't go away.

Instead, she thought of her mother. It surprised her to think that the idea of seeing Zanna again pleased her.

Might as well prod this a little, Calene thought.

She'd come face-to-face with her mother soon, for the first time in a decade. Anger lingered beneath the surface, but so did understanding.

I might not agree with what she did, Calene thought, *but I don't have a child. Do I know what I'd have done?*

All that time, she'd had Vettigan to speak to, to rely on. Losing him to the dark parasite had made her realise that her mother had no one like him in her life. Now, she yearned to apologise for all those years of silence. And to try to make amends. Calene understood she could have missed her chance, a thought that sent panic spiking through her chest.

Her relationship with Zanna *could* be mended, she

believed. Vettigan's damage appeared beyond her, but she hoped her mother's skill and knowledge could help. Her partner suffered, and even though she'd done her best to save him, her friend now felt like a stranger.

She shuddered as she brushed against Vettigan's consciousness. The darkness still lurked there, warping her friend's mind. Calene turned to watch him. He stood on the deck, facing the shore as they passed. He held a blanket tight across his back and chest and kept his hood up. He had smashed a mirror when he'd looked into it. Calene had felt their connection pulse with rage and grief as he looked on his grey skin and his lank, patchy hair.

"You should have left me to die," he'd growled when he awoke. Every time Vettigan looked at her, Calene heard those words.

She noticed the sailors eyeing the other passengers as they brought the ship home. *We're a droking odd-looking bunch, gods' teeth we are,* Calene thought, taking in her companions.

Brina stood with Tilo by the bulwark on the starboard side, a few paces from her, cloaked and hooded. The elf hid her hands beneath the folds of her clothing as the two talked, and Calene held no doubt that one gripped the hilt of her sword.

"This?" she heard Brina say, gazing around her. She'd taught Tilo a smattering of the common tongue, and he'd proven a willing and adept learner.

"Ship," the Banished replied, voice low so the deckhands wouldn't hear his accent. "Sea. Sky. Land."

"Good," Brina replied. "And me?"

"Elf," Tilo whispered. "Brina."

"Excellent. Now, what's—"

"Stop," Tilo commanded, holding out a hand.

He turned to the sea, gripping the rail as he gazed at the dock. He coiled, ready to explode into action, knuckles turning white. She wondered if standing on the deck bothered him. He hadn't ventured topside before that morning. Maybe he needed to vomit.

But, as they swept by an anchored vessel, she saw Tilo's head snap to watch it.

Calene did the same, and a cry escaped her lips as she saw a man stabbed multiple times in his chest and stomach. She clutched her chest as she felt his life dim with every plunge of the knife. Then the crew tossed him overboard like a sack of waste they were glad to be rid of. It all seemed to occur in slow motion; the way the body plummeted into the water as Tilo whipped off his cloak, unbuckled his weapons and dived in after the wounded man.

"Tilo, wait!" she yelled, slamming her hands on the rail.

It's like he knew it would happen, Calene wondered, as she peered over the rail to watch, grinding her teeth. *He could have warned us! Raas' teeth, why didn't he?*

She flicked her attention to the other ship. The attackers had already cleared their rail, leaving the man to die in the frigid water below. Unnoticed, Tilo swam with startling speed to the spot where the man had sunk and disappeared under the surface. Their vessel slowed, ready to dock, and Calene watched as the blue water turned red. Her stomach twisted when Tilo didn't emerge.

The boat lurched as it dropped anchor and slid to a stop. The crew hurled ropes out to the men on the pier to draw them in. Calene raced to the stern, Brina following, and watched the bloody water. The bubbles had disappeared, and now the waves sloshed undisturbed, the crimson stain dissipating.

"Raas, damn you," Calene growled, glancing at the statue of the god peering over the rooftops at them. Bitter bile rose in her gullet. "You could have done something, you lazy drok of a god. All this, just for Tilo to drown. For what? Brina, can you swim?"

"Nope," she said, watching the bloody water, "and I think someone would notice an elf leaping from a ship, don't you?"

"Drok!" Calene took a deep breath. She hated water, but she didn't see any other choice. Unbuckling her sword, she nodded, crushing her nerves with determination. She couldn't let Tilo drown. "See you on the other side."

"Look," Brina said, seizing her shoulder in a grip like iron and pointing below.

Calene gasped, relief washing through her, as Tilo's head burst from the murky water. He dragged a body, leaving a red trail behind it in the water. He reached the dock and lifted the stabbed man up towards the workers stationed there. They reached down and lifted the victim, then Tilo, onto the pier.

"Come on," Calene yelled, as the ship came to a full

stop and the deckhands lowered the gangplanks.

She sprinted across the deck towards the growing crowd.

This is going to be trouble.

◆

The crowd parted as Calene approached, Vettigan hobbling behind, muttering curses against Calene, elves, Tilo and the gods. Brina loitered at the back of the gathering, hood up and eyes narrowed. The dockworkers split their attention between the unusual appearance of the Banished and the unconscious, bleeding man lying face down on the pier.

Calene knelt beside him and put her fingers to his neck.

"There's a pulse," she said, to no one in particular, though she threw a glance at Tilo. He stared back. "Did you have to do that? I thought you'd died too."

"Liesh," he whispered, pointing at the dying man.

Calene rolled the stranger onto his front. His face tickled her memory, but a wheezing chuckle from Vettigan broke her concentration.

"What's so droking funny?" she growled.

"That," he said, thrusting a withered finger at the man, "is Master Kade Besem of the Haltveldt Conclave. Liaison to Solitude, to be exact. Someone must be unhappy with the job he's doing."

Besem? Calene thought, brushing the wet hair from his face. *Aye, that's him.*

She opened her Second Sight, drawing in the energy around her, preparing to heal him. Even though heat raced through her limbs from the stored magic, she rubbed her hands together to warm them before placing them on Kade's icy, bloody chest.

"You're adding another broken toy to our sorry little party?" Vettigan asked. "What's the point? If he dies, he dies."

"Drok off, Vettigan. Let me deal with this. Why don't you ask around, find out when the army passed through? We need to know if there are any Sparkers in town. Discreet, yeah?"

She pushed the healing magic into Kade. Tilo sang in a hushed voice, lending his power to hers. Without thinking, she reached out and drew it into her, as she did when she'd healed Vettigan after the Sparker attack. The Banished had covered his head with his wet cloak again as the onlookers started to gossip.

Calene scanned Kade's body. He'd suffered multiple stab wounds to his chest and torso; one had punctured a lung and another had nicked an artery, though none had pierced his heart. Lucky in that regard. She couldn't bring the dead back to life. Before seeing the Shadow Sparker's corpse rise to its feet, she hadn't thought anything could. Even so, the odds had been stacked against him. Blood loss and trauma would have killed him before he could drown. Tilo had acted in the nick of time.

She worked with speed, focusing on the bleed, the collapsed lung, the entry wounds before turning to the damage she noticed in his ankle.

Gods, did someone break it twice?

"Thanks, Tilo," she murmured without taking her stare from Kade. "Another thirty seconds and only Raas could have done anything for him."

"Happy with work," Tilo replied, in broken common. Calene smiled despite the situation. His improving grasp on Haltveldt's language made things easier.

To her Second Sight, her healing magic appeared blue within Kade's body, but the energy Tilo added looked a deep green. They merged together, like paint mixing. Different the magic might have been, but eager to fuse. The colours combined to create a vibrant yellow that flooded Kade's body, nourishing it, feeding it. Making it whole again. Calene marvelled at it. This hadn't happened when she'd healed Vettigan. She had the shadow parasite to thank for that.

Healing wounds like Kade's should have tested her, pushed her to her limits. Instead, she felt alive, full of strength and vigour. Healing a headache tested some Sparkers, and not many had the skill or power to bring someone back from the brink like that.

Kade coughed, watery bile gushing from his throat.

He looked up at her, baffled, and started to smile, before a convulsion shook him. He ground his teeth and arched his back, limbs snapping rigid. Tilo took Kade's head in a gentle but firm grip and held it in place, singing as he did.

Calene delved into Kade's body once more, easing

him into a deep sleep. He'd suffered so much damage. He needed to rest so his body, and mind, could absorb the healing.

"With my power and yours," Calene said, looking at Tilo, "he'll feel good as new in no time. I feel like I could heal him again without breaking a sweat. Don't know why the drok I'm talking out loud. You don't really understand what I'm saying, do you?"

"Yes. Some." Tilo grinned. He nodded at Kade. "Liesh".

"So you said."

She sighed. Glancing behind her, she saw Vettigan watching.

"I thought I asked you to scout?" she said, getting to her feet.

"So?"

"Raas damn you, Vettigan," Calene yelled, thrusting a shaking finger in his face. "What's your problem? You wanted to die, is that it? Well, I'm sorry. I couldn't leave you that way. No one else stood by me after what happened with my parents. You're my friend. No, you're my droking family! I did my best. I nearly drained myself dry for you. And I know it isn't enough and I know you deserve better and I know it *hurts* but... You have to try to fight it. Please?"

Waves sloshed around the pier and boats creaked. Calene glanced around. Brina had joined Tilo beside Kade, but the dockhands gaped at her, slack-jawed at her act of magic and her outburst. She ignored them and turned back to Vettigan. A shadow crossed his face and, for a moment, Calene readied herself for a fight.

"I just want my friend back," she whispered.

He sighed, features relaxing, scowl lifting. "You're right," he said. "It does hurt. But that's no excuse. I'm trying, Calene. Believe me. But it's like something's living inside me and it's turning me sour. It twists and perverts my thoughts. I can't feel the gods around me anymore and I'm afraid of what might happen if we Link. When I saw that man attacking Besem, this stain on my soul delighted in it. Like the violence and death called to it. It wants me to embrace my Spark. The very worst part of it. Calene, it terrifies me..."

Calene took his hands in hers and peered up at his face, under the hood.

How can I tell him that he's right? she thought, biting her lip as she thought of the shadow trapped on his brain, and the inky tendrils that put it there, forcing their way into his eyes and ears and mouth.

"Can you get us a cart?" she asked instead. "I'll talk to the dockhands, get the lay of the land. But we have to leave for Solitude as soon as we can. Maybe our friend can stop any bloodshed."

"And if he can't?" Vettigan muttered.

"Then I find my mother and we smuggle ourselves to Octaria or Avastia and we put Haltveldt as far behind us as we can. Zanna and I might have our differences, but I'm not leaving her to face a fight she can't win. And I think she might be able to succeed where I failed. She might be able to heal you."

Vettigan's shoulders shook. It took her a moment before she recognised it as laughter. He squeezed her hands and departed, drawing his hood tighter around his face.

"Right," Calene shouted, turning on the dockhands watching her. "Why so many people? Aren't you evacuating?"

The workers glanced at each other, trading confused looks. They refused to make eye contact with her. Before Calene lost her temper, a girl no more than fifteen stepped forward.

"Begging pardon, but why would we evacuate?"

"Spring Haven sent word, didn't they? The army's on its way?"

The girl looked like she wanted to dive into the water and swim as far away as she could. Somehow, she'd ended up as the mouthpiece for Adhraas harbour while the burly sailors and dockhands kept their silence. Calene thought about smiling, to calm her down, then remembered what Vettigan had said.

It's because your 'grin' resembles a lioness baring her teeth.

"No... I'm sorry. I'm not sure what you're talking about."

"The Banished," Calene yelled, and the girl flinched as she jabbed a finger at the Peaks of Eternity looming in the distance. "They're at Solitude's gates."

"We received word from Spring Haven," an older worker said, with a shrug. "The mayor said not to worry. The old Sparkers are telling tales. Politics, they said, that's all."

"You haven't heard?" Calene asked, shaking her head. "There are *thousands* of them. *Hundreds* of thousands. If they break through…"

"Raas save us," the man muttered, touching two fingers to his lips, then his forehead. Warding himself against trouble. "No lie?"

"I swear on my life, friend."

She turned, sweeping her eyes across the crowd, all staring at her. Listening. They'd seen her heal a near-dead man. They knew her as a powerful Sparker. In Adhraas, birthplace of the god who had given the gift, that alone carried authority. She just hoped it was enough.

"All that stands between you and the Banished is two hundred Sparkers! Spring Haven has left you to rot! Take what you can and abandon the rest! Go south, now! Raas be with you all!"

The man turned and ran. The others followed, the girl included. Calene stared after them, disbelief etched across her face.

Bells began ringing from the town centre, and she saw Vettigan pushing his way back through the crowd as they fled in rising panic.

"Calene," he said. "There's no droking evacuation. They're all carrying on as if Blessing Day's on the horizon. Working, drinking, carousing. Just living their lives."

"Not for long," she said, nodding after the departing workers.

"But that's not the worst of it," Vettigan said. "The army isn't marching."

"Is that a droking joke? Why?"

"Because the Emperor doesn't give a drok about anything other than finishing off the elves. Official word from Spring Haven is that Garet and Solitude are playing at politics, and want more coin. The mayor thinks Solitude are facing an army of a few dozen shepherds armed with sheep and pointy sticks."

"Arrogance," Brina snarled, appearing at Calene's elbow. "They'll pay for it once hundreds of thousands of Banished come flooding through Solitude."

"Janna blind them," Calene grunted. "The lot of them. Did you get that cart?"

Vettigan nodded. "This way."

"Brina, go with him. I'll help Tilo with our latest 'broken toy.'"

The elf squeezed her shoulder before moving away. Tilo watched the mountains.

He looks pensive, Calene thought, *but that's his home. He's never seen it from this angle.*

"Hey," she said, pointing at the sleeping Kade. "Help me with him?"

Calene mimed lifting, and Tilo nodded. She gasped as the warrior lifted him like a child, and slung him over one shoulder.

"Liesh," Tilo said, slapping Kade on the rump.

"So you keep droking saying. Let's go meet this purpose."

It took longer for them to get on the road than Calene would have liked. People packed the streets of Adhraas, jamming the roadways with carts and horses as word of the imminent Banished invasion spread, made all the worse by the fact that she'd started it all. The hours dragged by, testing her already-stretched patience, and afternoon arrived before they'd cleared the bustle of the frantic evacuation.

"Ten miles to Solitude," Calene muttered, flicking the horse's reins, though she understood the cart already moved as fast as it could. "We'll arrive by early evening. I hope it's soon enough."

She glanced at Vettigan, face hidden by the shadows of his hood. The flash of his old personality had sunk beneath the darkness again, and he'd spoken only in grunts since that morning.

"Calene," Brina said, climbing into the driver's seat beside her.

She still wore her cloak, but had removed the hood. It felt like the first time Calene could fully appreciate her beauty, after their talk aboard the ship from Colton. The antagonism had faded somewhat, leaving mystery and an eerie longing that Calene had never felt looking at a woman before.

She has a story to tell, Calene thought, meeting her emerald eyes and thinking of the elves they'd rescued on the road. *I hope to discover it. If she'll let me.*

The elf's fingers grazed hers, easing the reins from her hands. "I'll take over. Kade's awake. He won't talk to me. Just stared at me, eyes wide. Maybe it's because I'm an elf."

"Thanks."

She hesitated a moment, trying to think of something else to say, then hopped into the cart. Kade lay on the floor, Tilo watching him with a slight frown, as if the man were a puzzle the Banished hadn't figured out.

"Master Besem," Calene said, as she kneeled beside him. "Nice of you to make it all this way, but I think you forgot your army."

"Politics," Kade muttered, with a grimace. "You saved me?"

"I healed you," Calene corrected. "The Banished pulled you from the water."

Kade did a double-take, jaw hanging open. "A Banished? I thought him odd, but... Why is he here?"

"That's what we've been trying to find out. So far, all we've got is one word. 'Liesh'. Apparently, it's the elvish word for purpose."

"Liesh," Tilo stated.

"See? He's picked up a few common words since. Found him outside elven territory, down in a village near Colton. Basement of an inn, if you can believe it. No idea how he got there. But then, people showing up in strange places seems to be the norm these days. Aren't you supposed to liaise with Solitude from Spring Haven?"

Kade pushed himself up onto his elbows. His eyes flicked towards Brina's back and a shiver ran through him that Calene couldn't interpret. He busied himself staring at the skies.

"The Conclave wouldn't send an army, so I came."

"One man?" Calene laughed, glancing at the sky. It appeared darker than it should have at this hour. "Don't buy it. That isn't mentioning the seaman who tried to murder you, or the broken ankle you had before you even set foot on his ship."

"A friend and I tried to build a militia to take to Solitude. Master of War Nexes disagreed. They want a massacre. Like I said, politics."

Calene nodded. Pieces slotted into place. "We were attacked on the road, but they wanted the Banished. Sparkers, just like us. Well, not *exactly* like us. They had a new kind with them, called it a Shadow Sparker, and it won't be the only one."

"I feel like we've had our heads in the sand all this time. The Emperor's long planned for this. Like I said, they want a massacre. And it seems they're well-prepared for what comes after."

"So, you came all this way fleeing assassination by your own people too?"

Kade shook his head. She thought him handsome, in a sad way and if that type appealed. "My son," he whispered, "Arlo. He's apprenticed to a woman named Zanna at Solitude. I have to get to him.

"Zanna?" Calene dragged her hands over her face. "Teeth of the gods, this is too much..."

"I don't understand."

"Zanna is my mother."

"Liesh," the Banished said. He pointed at each person, as he said their name. "Tilo. Calene. Vettigan. Brina.

Kade." He glanced at Solitude. "Arlo. Liesh."

Tilo grinned at Calene. She ignored him, and the fact he'd left her mother's name from the list.

"Arlo," the Banished said, pointing at Brina. "Like elf. Same, almost. Not-same."

"How did you—" Kade started, but cut off as the earth trembled. A sound like thunder ripped through the black afternoon.

Calene spun and looked toward Solitude. She brushed against the Link she shared with her mother. For the first time in days, she felt something other than resolute focus. Anger, fear and panic overwhelmed her mother's consciousness.

"The Banished," she cried. "They're breaking through."

She flung herself to the front of the cart and grabbed Brina's shoulders.

"Go, as fast as you can, *please!* Raas, if you're listening, save us all."

CHAPTER THIRTEEN
SWEET SORROW

'Life, death. Laughter, sorrow. To kill, or to be killed. Black and white. We strive for another way.' - The words of Raas to Janna according to the holy scriptures. Their meaning, and context, are lost in the mists of time.

Carnage and confusion followed when the first section of Solitude's defence failed. Zanna witnessed the mistake as it happened; the Sparkers threw their energies and focus at filling the gap. That left other sections weak, and the Banished had counted on it. The attacks days before, the experimental volleys from their siege engines, had all been building to this.

The true offensive against Solitude began—arrows, stones, spears and boulders. Anything to weaken the barrier and topple the fortress's ramparts.

It worked. The Sparkers' magic faltered and the barrier blinked out, leaving those on the wall unprotected. Debris filled the air as projectiles crashed into the battlements, explosions of stone killing any defenders too slow to protect themselves.

Massive chunks of Solitude filled the trench below, allowing the Banished to storm the walls.

Through the deafening cacophony of their charge, the overlapping explosions and the crackle of magic, Zanna heard the screams of dying Sparkers and the roar of the Banished below. She turned to bark an order at Miriam, the woman she'd known for so long, and saw an arrow pierce her eye. She tumbled from the broken rampart and plunged into the attackers swirling below.

Another mage, Carron, screaming with fury, pulled in more energy than he could handle.

"Stop!" Zanna screamed, her warning swallowed by the raging battle.

Smoke billowed from Carron's ears as his anger turned to agony. She could see him lit up like a star with her Second Sight, continuing to suck in energy to feed his Spark. Zanna reached out to grab him, palms blistering from the heat where she touched.

"Carron!" she yelled, staring into his eyes. "Please, stop this! Let go!"

But he didn't see her. Didn't hear her. He'd lost himself in the Spark.

Carron's body vibrated, limbs convulsing. Blood poured from his ears as his brain turned to liquid. Tears blurred Zanna's vision as his screams turned to wet gurgles and bloody froth gushed from his mouth. With a sickening pop, Carron's eyes burst, black tears running down his cheeks.

Zanna looked away as he collapsed in a lifeless heap. He wouldn't be the last Sparker to burn out in the battle for Solitude's walls. Too much energy swirled around them, danced across the plains, calling for the Sparkers to use it, too much for many to handle.

Just days before, we said we'd defend, she thought, peering over the edge. *Now look. I was a fool to think Garet wouldn't act when I disobeyed him. He's pressed us into a battle we can't win. We'll all pay for this.*

The Sparkers had followed Garet's lead, raining fire, ice and lightning into the Banished's ranks. Bodies piled up against Solitude's walls, filling the trenches. The attackers climbed on them, using them to support ladders and ropes to assail the ramparts. In other places, they scrambled and died on the rubble from the chunks of stone blown from the top of the wall.

Zanna realised she hadn't seen her apprentice for hours.

"Arlo," she whispered, snapping out of the daze that had settled on her since Kearn's death. "This is no place for a child."

Garet had ordered her from the highest rampart earlier, but Arlo might have stationed himself there, as a message runner. She glanced up at the tower, bright with magic in her Second Sight.

If he's still alive, she thought, *Raas make it so.*

A ladder slammed into the ledge next to her. She spun, concentration broken, and before she could act, a surge of air whipped past her to push it away.

"Don't just stand there," a grizzled, old Sparker growled at her. Jasker, she thought. As weather-beaten as the stones themselves. "Droking useless bit—"

A rock arced over Zanna and smashed into Jasker's face. It exploded in a cloud of crimson.

Then, something changed. A subtle shift in the wind. A chill that made the hair on the back of Zanna's neck spring up.

The Banished screamed, their wails piercing the battle's clang of metal and cries of the dying, causing the Sparkers' magic to falter as they watched. They turned to face the Peaks of Eternity and the menacing colours hovering above them.

The maelstrom pulsed, ominous reds and greens and purples flickering out. Silence and darkness descended on Solitude as, for a moment, attackers and defenders stood as one and watched the horizon.

White light flashed, like the strangest lightning, to the tip of the highest peak, and its brilliance tore the sky apart. A deafening rumble followed. Zanna and her fellow Sparkers swayed. Some lost their footing as the quakes reached Solitude.

"Arlo saw this in his dream," she whispered, leaning on the battlements, wearied by the death all around. "The sky splitting... What can it mean?"

The Banished cried as one and charged, and the beam of mysterious light showed them rushing like an ocean toward the walls. Even the non-combatants, who had lingered behind the army for so long, plunged forwards.

They'd attacked with a calculated plan before. Now they surged in absolute panic.

———◆———

Calene could see Solitude in the distance, wedged between the Peaks of Eternity. The cart ate up the miles, rattling so hard she thought they might throw a wheel. The air shook with the sounds of battle—the pounding of boulders against the walls, the crackle and roar of magic, the screams of the dying. Louder and louder as they approached.

Even Adhraas would hear it by now.

"A mile, maybe two," she muttered, more to herself than anyone else.

Vettigan sat in the rear, but the rest of her group crowded the front seats, each face set in determination. Brina glanced at her, the strange lights illuminating the sky casting odd shadows across her face.

"Soon," she said, gripping Calene's forearm. "Patience."

"Why are you here?" Calene asked. "You could have slipped away. Boarded a ship for Octaria, Velen or Avastia. Anywhere. You know we'll all die, right?"

Brina bit her lip and glanced at Tilo. The Banished frowned at Solitude, tears in his eyes.

"Something tells me to stay near him, or at least bring him to Solitude in one piece. It's my...purpose." She met Calene's eyes and held them. "Besides, you're here."

Calene nodded. She felt the same way about Tilo, but hadn't wanted to admit it to herself. And she fought the sudden heat that bloomed from Brina's frank words and serious stare. Still, one question stood out.

The magic he wields. What is it?

When she gazed at him with her Second Sight, he appeared as any other Unsparked. But he'd done something to Vettigan—performed an aspect of sorcery that she couldn't—and the way her magic changed when mixed with his astonished her. She braced herself and reached out, measuring Vettigan's Spark, comparing it to her own. His seemed diminished, and she tasted its corruption, like drinking oily water. Meanwhile, she felt stronger than ever.

Had Tilo's power increased hers?

Without pausing, she swung her focus on Tilo and gasped. The Banished had no essence to measure.

Impossible, she thought. *Everyone has something, even if it's just energy to draw from.*

She pushed further. She felt the essence now, subtle and pure. He had the same feel as the trees at the roadside, the soil beneath, the horses and the wind. All the same. She'd never felt anything like it in a person before. Nature existed *through* him.

Tilo turned to stare at her, as if he'd noticed her prodding.

Calene went to ask Tilo to perform some kind of magic so that she could see it at work. Before she could speak, darkness devoured them. She heard screams echoing in the distance, then white light erupted on the horizon beyond

Solitude. The ground trembled and the monstrous percussion of the Banished's bombardment picked up again.

"It's in the air!" Vettigan yelled, rising to his knees in the back of the cart. "This madness, it calls to me! It pulsates within! Can't you feel it, Calene? Death welcomes us, and my Spark greets it!"

Tilo stood, threw off his cloak and unsheathed his sword. He sang, voice strong yet haunting, a lament filled with grief and rage.

"Il Renuish," he cried, lifting his sword above his head. "They come. Death."

Dread flooded Calene. She glanced at Vettigan, embracing her Second Sight, and shuddered. The shadow inside him, still ringed by Tilo's light, writhed. Its blackness seemed deeper than ever, as if the battle ahead strengthened it. Tilo's barrier pulsated, fighting to keep the parasite contained.

"Vettigan," Calene shouted over her shoulder, "that Evisceration changed you, and your Spark. Please, promise me you won't use it. For all we know, it could kill you."

It could kill us all.

Vettigan scowled, gave a petulant shrug and slumped back down.

"One thing's for sure," Kade said, staring at Tilo with his sword brandished over his head. "If he wanted us dead, he'd have killed us already. Something tells me the Banished aren't our enemy."

Calene pushed against her Link with her mother. She understood their relationship could never work the way it had. Long years of regret, anger and isolation had seen to that. But sensing her alive now brought her relief, and seeing the danger Zanna faced terrified her. Now they were separated only by Solitude's shadow.

You're my mother, she thought, sending her words through the connection, *and I won't let anyone hurt you. I'm coming. Hold on.*

———◇———

Zanna staggered up the stairs to the highest rampart, one hundred feet above the plains, scrambling on loose stones as the fortress shook. The Banished hurled themselves at the battlements, any thoughts of safe passage, of preserving life, forgotten. It could only be a matter of time before they overwhelmed the Sparkers on the walls.

As she opened the last doorway leading to the roof, Zanna froze as wind, cold and ferocious rain assailed her. She could see for miles around, could hear the shouts and screams both near and far. The plains heaved with movement. The Banished dragged their ranged weapons forward as they charged and continued their assault. Solitude's walls resembled broken teeth, and no doubt dead and dying Sparkers lay among the rubble.

Garet's plan had failed. His attack on the Banished who had come to talk in peace had sealed their fates.

There aren't enough Sparkers, she thought, gazing around at the mayhem. *A hundred more and we could have held. If Garet hadn't killed Kearn...*

Zanna saw faint lights in the far distance towards Adhraas. Boats moving into the clear seas. The town, evacuating. She sighed with relief.

She shook herself and focused on her task. The boy.

"Arlo," she cried, running up the open flight of stairs to the highest level.

A dozen Sparkers occupied the tower, several with swords drawn, magical flames licking the steel. In the gloom, the bright-robed magi with their weapons bared looked impressive, but Zanna knew most hadn't swung a blade in anger in years. Tired and forgotten old men and women were all Solitude had to offer. Still, they'd brandish steel and Spark together until their dying breath.

Gazing around, she discovered the smouldering husks of those who had burned out. An eyeless Sparker, still on her feet, staggered over the edge and plunged to her death.

"Master!" Arlo cried.

Zanna slid to her knees as her apprentice ran to her and gathered him up in her arms. She pulled away and held his pale, dirt-smeared face.

"Stay with me," she whispered, getting to her feet and taking his hand.

She saw Garet, hands behind his back, staring down at the throng below. Ladders and rappel lines bounced off the walls around him as Sparkers forced them back, but more appeared with alarming speed. Zanna strode towards him, Arlo close behind.

"Garet, you Raas-blind fool," she spat, slapping him with her full might as he turned to her. He fell to ground, looking up with shock. She glared at him. "You've killed us all."

"What would you have us do?" he snarled, defiance etched into his face. "Roll over and let the Banished stampede us? It's Adhraas next. We have to fight! *I* have to fight!"

"If we'd only *talked* to them—"

"Drok your talking," Garet snapped. "Haltveldt abandoned us to our fate. They've ignored us for years, and I accepted it. Showed my belly like a dog, because I understood what needed to happen down south, with the elves. All for the greater good. But this battle could prove our worth. Make the Emperor see us for what we really are. The defenders of his Empire. Imagine it, Zanna. Solitude no longer. They would name it Salvation, after us!"

Zanna heard warning shouts from the other Sparkers and moved on instinct. She seized Arlo and raised a shield as an enormous boulder slammed into the rampart, sundering the battlement and smashing the stone floor to rubble. Groans and wails told her not everyone had reacted with such speed.

"Are you safe?" she whispered, rolling off Arlo's body.

"Apart from standing in the middle of a battle, yes," the boy answered, with a weak laugh.

A ladder slammed into the gaping hole in the rampart, then another, followed by more. Zanna crawled forwards as the Sparkers that still breathed picked themselves up. She saw Garet lying nearby.

"Garet," she called. "Get up, if you can."

The Protector pushed himself up on his elbows with a scowl. When he looked beyond Zanna, his eyes snapped wide.

"No!" he screamed, surging to his feet.

For Zanna, it happened in slow motion. A Banished leapt onto the wall, mace in hand. Arlo faced him, small and frail in the darkness. Alone. The warrior raced towards him, weapon raised.

Then Garet charged at him, and black tendrils snaked from his raised hands. Zanna recognised it. Just as she'd reacted a decade ago, seeing her husband looming over Calene, Garet used Evisceration.

Isn't there a better way?

The black sorcery recoiled from the Banished and melted away, like a wave dashing to spray against a mighty cliff. Garet took an uncertain step back, staring at his hands.

"How—"

The Banished lunged and brought his mace down on the Protector's head in a mighty overarm swing. Zanna stared, helpless, as the weapon crushed Garet's skull like a watermelon. The first blow drove him to his knees, then the Banished swung again for good measure.

More attackers reached the walls, and the defenders who could rushed to meet them with swords and Spark.

Arlo stood rooted to the spot, a small shape adrift in an ocean of fire, destruction and death.

"Sure you're up to this?" Calene murmured to Kade, as they approached the fortress. Sounds of battle threatened to deafen. "You can stay down here. I'll get my mother and the boy and bring them straight out."

"How do you know where they are?" Brina asked, gazing up at Solitude. She opened her mouth to say more, then appeared to think better of it.

She thinks they're dead, Calene thought.

She glanced at Kade, who watched the looming battlements moving closer and closer. Brina whipped the reins, urging the horses on to the verge of collapse.

"He's my son," the man said, full of conviction. "I've abandoned him once. I won't do it again."

"Right," Calene muttered. "Just stay in the middle of us. You're in no condition to fight. It's a wonder you're awake after the amount of healing I had to do. Do you even have a weapon?"

Kade grimaced. "Threw my sword at someone. Only way I could escape Spring Haven."

"Well," Brina called, pulling the cart to a halt, "we're about to head into a battle. I'm sure you'll find a weapon lying around somewhere."

The party leapt down, drawing swords in unison. The cacophony above drowned out the sound of the steel— screams of the dying and desperate, the crumbling of the defences, the roar of magic and siege. Calene smelled the thick stench of charred bodies in the air. She looked at Vettigan, standing glassy-eyed, sword twitching. Blue flames, tinged with darkness, inched their way up the blade.

"A massacre," he breathed. "I feel all their deaths. Inside me. Calling to me."

Calene gripped his shoulder. "I warned you. No droking Spark, remember?"

"You need me. Look at your army."

She snarled. "Fine. You stay up front with me. Brina, you and the Banished take the rear. Kade, get in the middle."

She turned to face the group. *Broken toys, Vettigan called us. We're here for a reason. Liesh.*

"Wait here while I get my mother's attention. Then, we move."

Calene closed her eyes and focused on the Link with her mother. She sucked in her will, her fear and anger. Desperation and love. She used all the energy that swirled around Solitude—so much, so strong!—and drew it into her, holding it tight. A ghost of a smile flickered on her lips as she thought of Tilo's favourite word: purpose.

Mother, she projected, unleashing her emotions towards the gateway in her mind where Zanna connected.

A gong sounded in her head. Light flashed behind her eyes; she pictured the obsidian wall separating them crumble at her command.

Calene? I'm so sorry, but—

I know you're under attack. We're here, mother. Outside the walls.

No! No, Calene. Get away from here. Now! I can't lose you. There's been so much death already.

My thoughts exactly. I'm coming to get you and I'm

alone. The boy, Arlo, too. His father is with us.

The exchange lasted seconds, but the relief and love that washed over Calene filled her to the brim.

He's with me, Zanna replied, *the highest level. Through the gate, up the stairs, as high as you can go. Thank you, Calene.*

Meet us.

We're losing the walls. I can't leave—

The connection broke off as Zanna's focus switched elsewhere. Calene reached out for her, like groping in the darkness. Her mother lived still, but she couldn't respond.

"Pleasant news, I know where they are," she said, turning to Solitude's gates. "Unpleasant news, sounds like it's the epicentre of the fighting. The plan is simple. Get in, get my mother and Arlo, leave. I don't know what purpose the Banished had, but it's too late for that now. Brina, make sure Tilo keeps that droking cloak on and his hood up so a Sparker doesn't incinerate him. They've unleashed themselves and we don't want him caught in the crossfire."

"Tilo's purpose all important," the Banished grunted, in his broken way. "War happen. Can't stop. Muir can."

"If a droking rock can stop this," Calene said, staring up at the smoke billowing from the top of the walls, "it's welcome to try. Follow me."

She raced forward, glancing behind her just long enough to see the others fall into place. Vettigan kept pace with her, features grim.

"Can I count on you?"

"Death calls to me," he breathed, reaching the portcullis and opening a door to the tower's stairwell, "but I can't let you down. I have to remember that. You're everything I have too, child."

Calene gripped his arm and wished things could go back to how they were. Only days had passed, but it felt like years. Years of running, fighting, hiding from their own people. Years of a wall between them, severing their Link, like a missing piece of her.

They ascended the stairs, stumbling as the fortress shook from repeated impacts. Sweat poured from Calene's forehead despite the chill, stinging her eyes, as she took two steps at a time. As they passed a window looking out on the path they'd arrived on, a violent tremor knocked her from her feet. She slammed into Vettigan, who slipped a few steps down and collided with the others.

As they lay there, she heard voices above. Banished voices.

"Drok," Calene growled, pushing herself to her feet. "Get ready."

Four Banished appeared above them on the stairs. They paused, taking in Calene's party. She could see doubt flash in their pale eyes; her crew didn't look like Sparkers. Her gaze flicked to the heavy mace carried by the leader. She half-turned, about to call for Tilo to reveal himself, and the Banished charged.

Vettigan leapt in front of her, deflecting the Banished's weapon with his sword. Sparks flew as the blade and mace dragged across the wall. Calene rushed forward as they wrestled on the narrow, twisting stairwell. The tight space made swordplay awkward and now she regretted not carrying a dagger. Another Banished swung a handaxe at her and she ducked, steel chipping the stone. Snarling, she drew her arm back, ready to strike.

A hand grabbed her from behind, yanking her out of the way. Tilo danced by, knocking Vettigan back as he raised his sword to deliver a death blow. His hands moved in a blur as he engaged his fellow Banished, grabbing wrists, twisting weapons loose and letting them clatter to the floor, sweeping legs and dropping them to the stones.

Within seconds, he had the four Banished defeated. He loomed over them, and removed his hood.

"Tilo!" one of them gasped, face shifting from anger to disbelief to wonder in the blink of an eye. "Ma heran?"

"Vah," Tilo replied, pointing up the stairs then back at Calene and her dumbstruck companions. "Liesh."

He stooped, and pulled the other man to his feet. Another rumble rocked Solitude. The wasted seconds made Calene's teeth ache. Tilo embraced his kin, then scooped a discarded sword from the floor and held it out to Kade, who took it but kept his wary eyes on the Banished.

"Brient gur so, reen." Tilo pointed back down the stairs.

The warrior nodded, signalled to his companions and pushed his way past Calene, eyes lowered as he did.

"What did you tell them?" Calene asked, watching them flee.

"Tell them run. Tell them we have liesh."

"Of course," Calene grunted. She glanced at her

friends. "Come on. And pull your hood up, Tilo."

She raced up the last few steps and flung the door open. The furious sounds of battle hit her like a gale. She stood on a lower level, with more stairs leading to the top.

"Drok," Vettigan spat behind her.

Her limbs shook as she gazed around. Solitude had become a ruin. Bodies lay strewn, crushed by rubble or stabbed, bludgeoned, burned in the conflict atop the wall. But the chaos went well beyond the fortress. Smoke rose from the Banished's plain and thousands of dead filled trenches at the foot of the walls. Hundreds of thousands more, still living, surged towards Solitude, an ocean of blackness sweeping the land below. No details, no faces, just a churning mass of bodies animated by blind panic. How had so many Banished hid up here all these years?

Looming over it all, the white column of light linking the inky sky to the mountain's highest peak—defying nature and the gods—weakened her bladder.

She opened her Second Sight. Tiny beacons of magic dotted the fortress' lower levels, but the largest concentration manned the pinnacle. She focused on it, brushed against the Link in her mind, and knew her mother fought there. Calene bounded up the stairs and her heart leapt into her mouth when she finally laid eyes on Zanna.

Her mother fought a Banished, sword against sword. A small boy stood in her shadow, tiny body sagging as he stared out at the Peaks of Eternity and the pure, white pillar rising from it, like he had no comprehension of the battle raging around him. Dead and burned-out Sparkers, dozens of Banished and the remains of Solitude's battlements lay strewn across the floor. Attackers swarmed the walls from ladders leaning against the gaping holes in the ramparts, and only a handful of defenders remained to meet them.

Calene wanted to scream to her mother, but knew she couldn't break her concentration. She felt a surge of pride seeing her fighting without the power of Evisceration, though it put her life at risk.

Calene heard heavy footsteps behind her as Brina, Kade and Tilo joined them. She glanced at Vettigan and bared her teeth. "Into battle, old friend?"

"Wait!" he called, before she could charge into the melee. He snatched at her sword arm. "I can end it all, with the Spark. I feel so full of power! I can stop them in their tracks. Save everyone!"

"No droking Spark," she snapped, staring at his ruined face, into his dark, hooded eyes. Just days before, he'd appeared so noble. So caring. Now, he scowled back at her. "I can see the stain inside you, Vettigan. It's alive, and all this death is feeding it. Fight it. Please."

A growl escaped him, then he threw his head back and howled into the black sky. "I can't, Calene... It's too much. The power to save you all... It's right there, within my grasp."

Teeth clenched, her old friend convulsed. Dark energy overwhelmed her senses and it came from him, swelling until it felt ready to explode. She scanned him with her Second Sight and saw the black parasite on his brain had overcome Tilo's light, shattering the barrier, and spreading to fill up the rest of his body.

"Stay away from him!" Zanna's scream pierced the din of the battle, drawing Calene's eyes to her.

A Banished broke off from the fighting and ran at Arlo, still staring out at the Peaks of Eternity, oblivious to the carnage and chaos. Calene recoiled as the darkness within Vettigan bloomed until it turned overpowering. Maybe she couldn't save him, but she *had* to save the boy. She charged forwards to meet the Banished.

Zanna dispatched her opponent with a pommel-strike to the head and threw herself in front of the boy.

———◆———

Kade followed Calene through the doorway and choked at the carnage spread out before him.

Please be alive, he thought, gazing at the broken battlements and fallen defenders. *Raas, please make it so.*

Then he saw him.

Arlo. Bigger than before he'd been sent to Solitude, but still tiny and still very much a child. A child whose father never should have sent him to such a far-flung place. To the middle of a warzone. Kade's heart sang at the sight of him—his son, still alive, within his grasp.

Except that Arlo seemed there in body only. He stared at the distant mountains, paying no heed to the Banished moving to cut him down. A Sparker, exhaustion etched into her features, screamed and threw herself forward, but

Kade knew she wouldn't make it in time.

"Arlo!" Kade cried. He hurled his sword, like when he'd confronted Nexes.

This time, he didn't miss.

The blade cut through the air, past Calene who raced to meet the Banished, straight through the attacker's throat. The warrior flew backwards as another surged forward in his place. This time, Calene met him, their swords ringing against each other.

"Vettigan, no!" the Sparker, Zanna, screamed.

Kade saw the old Sparker with his head thrown back, eyeballs rolling to their whites in his head, tongue lolling.

Fear and disgust etched into Zanna's face as she stretched her arms towards Vettigan. Kade glanced at Brina, who appeared paralysed with indecision, head twisting between Calene and Vettigan.

"I need to protect my son," Kade whispered, taking a step toward Arlo.

Something heavy crashed into him from behind and knocked him to the floor.

<hr />

Zanna felt the terrible energy building up within Vettigan. It eclipsed everything atop Solitude's walls.

She knew that Calene stood over Arlo, fighting a Banished warrior for his life. She knew that Kade had arrived for his son, that an elf and a Banished stood as part of Calene's party, but Vettigan stole her focus.

With her Second Sight, she watched a black shadow pulsating inside him, then forcing its way out. Tendrils of oily darkness oozed from his ears, eyes, nostrils and throat. It writhed, alive, and it called to her. She sensed its power, and the invading presence seemed to respond to her. Her Spark far outstripped Vettigan's. It whispered to her.

She knew she could call on the miasma, take possession of it, use it to vanquish the Banished and wreak exquisite death on anything or anyone that attacked her.

"No..." Zanna whispered, glaring at the shadow. "You can't tempt me. I am beyond you."

The parasite swirled in response, billowing larger as Vettigan lurched, arms rising skyward, fingers curling into claws. It pulsated around him, holding shape but quivering like a dam ready to burst, but still it drew more to it, feeding on all the death, agony, rage and desperation surrounding them, almost reaching breaking point.

"Shield yourself!" Zanna cried, her face coated with blood and sweat.

She raised her magical barrier, hoping Calene heard her and reacted in time. She threw herself at Vettigan as the hooded Banished shoved past Kade and the elf and lunged at Arlo, covering him with his body. She felt Calene's Spark, strong and bright, and realised with relief that she had heard the warning.

Vettigan howled—a scream filled with fury, pain and madness. A wave gushed out from him, oozing tendrils snaking out towards Banished and defenders alike. He had no control over it. The shadow wanted only one thing.

Death.

Zanna's shield reached Arlo and the Banished, just as the tide of shadow hit.

Lightning danced inside the pulsating darkness as it caught the mass of bodies atop Solitude's walls and swept them from the ramparts like a tidal wave, carrying them down into the chaos below. Wind howled around them, pelting them with ash and bloody rain. Zanna clenched her teeth and dug her toes into the stone as the impact rocked her backwards. She saw the Banished slipping towards the broken edge, Arlo clung to his chest.

Her shield lessened the initial assault—she heard the screams of the unshielded Sparkers and Banished as the shadow hit them, smelled their flesh burn as the lightning seared them—but the evil battered at her protection. It wanted her soul, to feed on her Spark until nothing remained, and it wouldn't stop until it succeeded.

Calene crawled towards Vettigan, clinging to her own magical shield. The Banished she had fought had turned to a fused puddle at her feet as the darkness ate every scrap of life in what had once been its body. She still clutched her sword and aimed it at him, her oldest friend, who just cried with mad, howling laughter.

He pulsated in Zanna's Second Sight. The death the miasma caused added to his strength, his Spark, but he could only hold so much. Soon, he'd burn out and take everyone on the rampart with him. In fact, a power like that might wipe out every soul on the plains below once untethered from Vettigan's body.

It had ended the battle, but it wouldn't stop until they were all dead.

Kade fought to get to his feet, inching towards Arlo, when a gust of hellish wind swept him up and slammed him into the elven woman. They crashed into the far wall and Kade flipped over it. The elf reached out in time, grabbing his arm as he hung over the side. The wind lifted him horizontal, threatening to hurl him all the way to Adhraas. The woman clung to him with all her strength, screaming through gritted teeth.

Zanna heard those screams. And she heard the cries of the dying, the wounded and the terrified. She felt the fading embers of hope from those around her as Vettigan's dark magic oozed over the ramparts and spilled onto the Banished below.

All this death, she thought, *but there's always another way.*

She stared at Calene. How she'd longed for this day, to gaze upon the daughter she hadn't seen for ten years. When she'd grieved alone for what she'd done to her husband, for what her actions had meant to their child, she'd yearned for one more chance to tell her she loved her, that she hadn't meant to hurt her.

Zanna looked at the woman her daughter had become without her—brave, strong, capable. A woman who fought for her friends. Vettigan, Kade, an elf, a Banished... All to stop this mindless destruction and rescue her and Arlo.

She regretted the time she'd wasted—the moments

they'd never have, never share—but shoved it aside. Instead, she focused on the memories that comforted her during the long nights alone in Solitude. The times when she taught Calene to read, her daughter's endless curiosity as she asked questions about Raas, Janna, and the Spark. Her kind soul, when she always insisted that another way existed, that their gift wasn't just a weapon.

Pride surged in her chest, and she threw her focus to Calene for a second. Her daughter glanced at her, and their eyes met.

I love you.

Zanna let her shield fall and allowed the energies swirling around Solitude to flow into her.

Always.

Tears stung Calene's eyes as her mother's words rushed through her. The weight of emotion staggered her and, in a moment of horrifying realisation, she knew why.

She's saying goodbye.

Still struggling towards Vettigan, she flung her arm out to Zanna, as all the words she hadn't spoken ran through her mind. The regrets, the anger, yes. But the warmth she felt for her, the excitement at seeing her again too. She wanted to tell her that she forgave her, wanted to fall into her arms and be held, the way her mother had held her years before. To feel safe, loved and protected in a way only her mother could make her feel.

Right then, Calene knew those things and more would remain forever unsaid. She wanted to fall to her knees, to scream them out, but she had to reach Vettigan. Stop him before he killed *everyone*.

Calene tried to send a message back, one she hoped would carry through the maelstrom, but her Link told her Zanna's focus had turned elsewhere.

Her body transformed into a bright light against the darkness. Calene saw the air around her dance with energy as it flooded into her, like moths racing to the only flame for miles around. She flung her arms wide and lifted off her feet, enveloped in the purest Spark Calene had ever seen.

Into the howling maelstrom, she cried, "I love you."

<hr />

And Zanna heard her, cutting through the chaos, urging her on in this final act.

Not enough, Zanna thought, willing more energy into her body. Then, she remembered the words of her daughter, the same ones she told Arlo days earlier.

Magic is a partnership. It's so simple once you figure that out.

Partnership meant trust. It meant understanding. It meant mutual surrender. She couldn't *use* the Spark. She had to work with it. She relaxed and let her senses expand. She discovered flame and water, life and death, destruction and hope. Creatures burrowing beneath the earth, and some flying, high in the sky. Zanna experienced regret and rebirth, but still she sent her senses out further. Something called to her, that curiosity lingering in the tallest spire of the Peaks of Eternity. The presence she'd noticed earlier when she met Kearn before Solitude's gates, older than the stones of Solitude, even than those of the mountain that housed it.

The rock. The Lodestone Arlo had rediscovered. It welcomed her, embraced her, and fed its energies into her.

Surrender doesn't mean defeat, child. There is always another way.

The voice reverberated in her mind, calming her even as it filled her with strength. The gods spoke to her.

Raas?

I see you. I have always seen you, daughter. Open yourself. Trust in me and I shall guide you. Your goals are noble, fitting for one with your gift. Surrender.

Zanna smiled, opened her eyes and let the Spark flow through her.

"How are you doing this?" Calene cried, staring at her mother, astounded by her power.

No one could hold so much but she knew the answer. A green column flowed from the distant mountains into Zanna, just like when Tilo had aided her with his song. The Banished's magic seemed a stream compared to the ocean pouring from the Peaks of Eternity.

She fought her way to Vettigan, but the wind grew stronger, the storm of darkness a torrent, with only Zanna's light illuminating them. His eyes stared, but what he saw Calene couldn't guess. She had to end this, before he fumbled what little mastery of the dark magic he had, burnt out and took this whole chunk of Solitude with him.

If—when—he lost control of that evil, who knew how much more destruction it would cause on the Banished below and any Sparkers who still lived?

She glanced again at Zanna, squinting through the gale, the dark shadow beating against her shield. Her mother floated above the rampart, the murderous miasma curling away from her, the green now emanating from within.

She should have gone supernova, Calene thought, inching forward, *but she's getting stronger. How long can she do this alone?*

"No," she growled to herself, teeth gritted. "She doesn't have to do it alone."

Careful not to drop her shield, Calene drew on her own energy, her essence, and let it out into the blizzard of energy. Just a slither, but she imbued it with the unspoken feelings she had longed to voice—her love, pride, and strength. A smile broke out across Zanna's serene face.

She feels it! Calene laughed, tears wetting her cheeks.

Her mother's gentle touch caressed her as she accepted the sacrifice and, at that moment, Calene comprehended the magnitude of her mother's actions. The energy she pulled into her body, the light she held, and more. For a second, she noticed another presence, ancient and vast. A guiding hand for a true believer.

Calene laughed, falling to her knees, but her joy turned sour. As she gazed at her mother, inching forward, she saw a shape materialise out of the gloom. A boulder the size of a townhouse hurtled towards them, moments away with no escape.

The Banished, trying to end the threat of the darkness that promised to consume them all.

"We're droked. Damn you Raas, and your rotten, stinking teeth."

Helpless, she stared at the ruins surrounding her, the corpses by her feet. At Vettigan, still howling with mad laughter and boiling over with dark malice. At Tilo, huddled over Arlo, protected by Zanna's shield but sliding towards the edge. At Brina, holding onto Kade for dear life as he hung into empty air, the wind pulling him from her grasp. At her mother, that shining beacon bright against the darkness.

Calene closed her eyes, and wished she could have hugged Zanna one last time, could listen to her sing again. She wished she knew for certain she'd heard when Calene told her she loved her.

The boulder slammed into Solitude, the stones exploding beneath her feet. Calene flew forward, saw Kade fall from the wall, dragging Brina with him. Spinning as she fell through the air, she saw Tilo topple too, spilling over the side with Arlo in his arms.

Her motion stopped as time slowed to a crawl.

Vettigan's spell winked out with a sudden rush of air and a pop. She didn't fall through the air like a rag doll anymore. Instead, an unseen hand lifted her. Calene recognised the feeling—a bubble of protective magic, like the ones her mother used to create for her to practice her Spark. Vettigan floated beside her, unconscious, the stones of Solitude falling away beneath them, crumbling as the boulder obliterated the tower.

She gasped and watched as Tilo and Arlo floated above the Banished army, while Kade and Brina drifted on the other side, saved from their fall. The same bubble that caught her held them and slowed their motion. She laughed, tears in her eyes.

Other Sparkers lifted from the lower ramparts, too. Calene embraced her Second Sight and saw luminous green bubbles, the same colour that emanated from Zanna, surrounding them, lifting every living soul from Solitude's walls, protecting them. It all happened in the space of a second, but to Calene, time stretched. She looked at her mother, who gazed back, face full of beauty and warmth.

There's always another way, Zanna's voice projected in her mind, as she pushed out with her arms.

As Calene floated backwards, she saw the Banished's siege weapons crumble on the plain below before she sank out of view.

Thank you, my child.

The light in her mother burst outwards, turning Calene's vision white before she could raise a hand to protect her eyes. She felt herself landing on the soft ground as the earth cracked and groaned around her. Then she faded into darkness.

———◇———

Calene blinked. White spots danced in her vision. She reached out and felt a body lying beside her. Running her hands across it, her fingers came across a familiar beard.

"Vettigan?" she hissed. "Can you hear me?"

She lowered her head to his chest and relaxed when she heard a heartbeat.

"Brina?" she called, lifting her head. "Kade? Anyone?"

Wind whistling through the trees answered her. She rubbed her eyes and peered at her surroundings.

"Drok..." she muttered, heart lurching up her throat. "Raas have mercy."

Solitude had disappeared. In its place lay a wide canyon, severing the Banished from Haltveldt and the south. Across the gap, Calene saw them milling around, picking themselves up, tending to the wounded and the dead. Confused yells mixed with disbelief drifted across to her. She opened her Second Sight and spotted several beacons of magic on her side of the ravine. Sparkers, safe and sound, though she reckoned less than thirty had survived.

She gazed across the canyon, and her Second Sight picked up another beacon. A child, but one with strength she'd never seen in one so young, his Spark so immense it staggered her that she hadn't noticed it before. She closed her eyes and focused on it.

Something tugged at her Sight, a familiar presence next to the beacon. A presence with life and nature flowing together as one. Tilo.

Calene scanned her surroundings, wondering where Kade and Brina had landed, hoping they'd stayed safe, but she could see no sign of them. She worried what her fellow Sparkers might do if they stumbled upon an elf.

You saved us, mother, Calene thought, *and you found another way. The Banished will still cross, but now we've time to find out what they want. You've bought us the chance to avert a war.*

"Are we alive?" Vettigan muttered. Calene turned to him. He lay staring up at the sky, tears streaming down his face.

"Yes," she said, lacking the energy to put heat into her voice, "no thanks to you. Mother sacrificed herself to save everyone. For now."

"Calene," he whispered. "I don't know what happened. I remember voices, calling to me. So many. And power. Power enough to save us all, but then... Nothing. I can't remember anything after that. The Spark, I can't feel it. It's gone. I feel so...empty."

She took his hand in hers. "Our friends are gone too. Brina and Kade are missing. I saw them lifted as they fell, but I've no idea where they landed."

"The Banished, Tilo?"

"He's with Kade's boy. Over there." She tossed her head to where Solitude had once stood, now nothing but a yawning chasm between the Peaks of Eternity. "Somewhere we can't reach."

Vettigan pushed himself up and gasped as he looked

across the canyon. The unnatural darkness faded to a normal one, and a green spire of light towered over where the fortress had been, answering the white one in the distance.

"What do we do?" Vettigan asked, turning to Calene.

"Purpose," she whispered. "We discover what it is, and we don't rest until we do. There's more to all of this, and I intend to figure it out. But first, we find our friends. Tilo and the boy are on the other side, but Kade and Brina need us. And we tell everyone, Vettigan. We tell them all what Zanna Alpenwood did here. We tell them that the Empire left them to die, and she saved us, and if it's the last thing I ever do, I'll discover what the Banished want, Raas' teeth, so I will."

She climbed to her feet, holding out a hand to him. It hung there between them. He refused to meet her eyes, but she didn't pull away and he reached out, brushing his fingers against hers, then gripped her hand. Calene heaved him to his feet and they turned together, watching the shimmering, emerald light touch the heavens. The mournful, haunting voices of the Banished drifted to them in the wind, singing.

"Come on," Calene said, gripping Vettigan's shoulder. "We've got work to do."

As her friend sighed and turned away, she looked back at the empty space that had once been Solitude.

Goodbye, mother, Calene thought, forcing back tears. *We'll meet again, Raas and Janna willing.*

She followed Vettigan, determined to find Brina, Kade and the truth, and left Solitude's shadow behind her.

EPILOGUE
THE RETURN

Malek watched the battle from the tallest point of the Peaks of Eternity. The balcony built into the cliff face offered a commanding view of Solitude. Or it had.

A spectacular display of magic, he thought, thinking of the blaze of energy that had eradicated the fortress. *These barbarians are capable of grand feats.*

He turned and strode across the focus chamber, pausing by the Lodestone and gazing at the full, lush tree growing from it. He reached a hand out, then pulled away. It didn't pulse with such life in *his* world, but Malek had witnessed what the source could do to those who didn't respect it. The Lodestone didn't like to be touched.

"In my world, you're almost dead," he told it. "In fact, using you to come here killed you. Imagine what we can do together now, with you so healthy. So vibrant and powerful. You still have so much to achieve before you serve your purpose."

He made his way to the rear balcony. The white portal beacon reached down from the sky to touch the ground on the other side of the Peaks, spreading hundreds of feet wide. Its edges shimmered as his armies passed through and assembled on the cold and desolate plains. Hundreds of thousands of fighting men and women. His vanguard.

Magi toiled on the other side of the portal, where his home lay. He could see glimpses of it—the blood-red sky of a dying world. The magi assured him they had the time and the power to transport his people, his Emperor, to safety, but they'd been wrong before. Very wrong.

In aeons to come, a city would grow in the spot where his army assembled. A place that would become Malek's city, the home of his Emperor. He gazed across the centuries and thought of the fires, floods and earthquakes that had devoured his world.

This Haltveldt is ripe for the taking, Malek thought, turning away and letting his gaze fall on the Lodestone. *And once we've purged this continent, the world will be ours.*

THE END.

David Green is a writer of dark fiction. Born in Manchester, UK and living in Galway, Ireland, David grew up with gloomy clouds above his head, and rain water at his feet, which has no doubt influenced his dark scribblings. David is the author of the Pushcart Prize nominated novelette Dead Man Walking, and is excited for his fantasy series, Empire of Ruin, debuting in June 2021 from Eerie River Publishing.

Newsletter: https://tinyurl.com/y6ah8brp
www.twitter.com/davidgreenwrite
www.davidgreenwriter.com
https://www.facebook.com/davidgreenwriter

COMING 2021

PATH OF WAR:
EMPIRE OF RUIN BOOK TWO

**THE BANISHED HAVE MADE THEIR MOVE,
NOW HALTVELDT ANSWERS BACK.**

Reeling from the events at Solitude, Calene Alpenwood
embarks on a journey to find meaning in all that she's
seen, and discover the answers she so desperately seeks.
Finding herself more alone than ever, Calene is
trapped between doing what's right, and doing what
needs to be done.

Meanwhile, Kade Besem continues his search for his son,
Arlo, and the strange warrior-monk Tilo. His hunt
takes him deep into Banished territory and into
the jaws of danger.

Revelations are revealed, ancient secrets are uncovered
and those who stand in the Empire's way can't hope to
win when Haltveldt walks the *Path of War*.

WWW.EERIERIVERPUBLISHING.COM/EMPIRE-OF-RUIN

ALSO BY DAVID GREEN

Brand New Adventures with Nick Holleran Series

Nick Holleran, private detective, had seen it all.
Then he died and returned to life, realizing he understood
a lot less than he thought. He saw Heaven, waiting above,
but discovered there's no Hell below - the living reside
there already, oblivious to the ghosts, demons, and fallen
angels amongst us.

Taking cases to earn his way a ticket into Heaven and
to discover the truth of the world surrounding him, a
job falls into Holleran's lap that brings his past into the
present, testing his new found virtues. Revenge is a sin,
and sinners spend all their lives in Hell.

For Nick Holleran, work is Hell; but you can't keep a
dead man down.

DEAD MAN WALKING - JULY 2021
THE DEVIL WALKS IN BLOOD - JULY 2021

FROM EERIE RIVER PUBLISHING

NOVELS
In Solitude's Shadow
Sentinel
Storming Area 51

ANTHOLOGIES
Don't Look: 12 Stories of Bite Sized Horror
It Calls From The Forest: Volume I
It Calls From The Forest: Volume II
It Calls From The Sky
It Calls From The Sea
Darkness Reclaimed
Midnight Shadow: Volume I
With Blood and Ash
With Bone and Iron
Forgotten Ones: Drabbles of Myth and Legend
Dark Magic: Dark Fantasy Drabbles

COMING SOON
Path of War
It Calls From the Doors
It Calls From the Veil
The Void
A Sword Named Sorrow

www.EerieRiverPublishing.com

Don't Miss Out!

Looking for a FREE BOOK?
Sign up for Eerie River Publishing's monthly newsletter
and get **Darkness Reclaimed** as our thank you gift!

Sign up for our newsletter
https://mailchi.mp/71e45b6d5880/welcomebook

Here at Eerie River Publishing, we are focused on
providing paid writing opportunities for all indie authors.
Outside of our limited drabble collections we put out each
year, every single written piece that we publish -including
short stories featured in this collection have been paid for.
Becoming an exclusive Patreon member gives you
a chance to be a part of the action as well as giving you
creative content every single month, no matter the tier.
Free eBooks, monthly short stories and even paperbacks
before they are released.

https://www.patreon.com/EerieRiverPub

Made in the USA
Columbia, SC
26 January 2022

54813895R00162